Wicked In Bed

Sheri Campbell

The
X
Press

Published by:
The X Press
PO Box 25694
London N17 6FP

Tel: 020 8801 2100
Fax: 020 8885 1322
Email: vibes@xpress.co.uk

This edition published 2001
Copyright © Sheri Campbell 1995

Printed by Ominia Books.

Distributed in UK by Turnaround Distribution, Unit 3, Olympia Trading Estate,
Coburg Road, London N22 6TZ
Tel: 020 8829 3000
Fax: 020 8881 5088

Distributed in US by LPC Group, 1436 West Randolph Street, Chicago, Illinois 60607, USA
Orders 1-800 626 4330 Fax orders 1-800 334 3892

ISBN 1-874509-14-X

ABOUT THE AUTHOR

Born in Hackney, east London, of Jamaican parents, 29-year-old Sheri Campbell is a legal secretary for a law firm in the City. She has also written the bestseller *Rude Gal*, and is currently working on her new novel *Down & Nasty*. She is 'single by choice' and lives in a loft apartment in Shoreditch.

ONE

The robotic voice of the announcer repeated the message for a second time.

"Will all passengers for flight BA374 to Kingston, Jamaica please make their way to departure gate 15 immediately."

Heathrow airport seemed especially busy this Monday morning and Michael Hughes had been trying with limited success to get 'the love of his life' through the main departure gate.

He looked at his Rolex then towards the entrance of the Harrods airport boutique. Terminal 4 had certainly changed since the last time he had been there. Designer name boutiques were now everywhere and he knew that it would spell trouble with this female and for his tight itinerary. As he paced back and forth outside the store, she emerged with green ribboned boxes laced around her fingers and a credit card in her mouth.

"Nadia, is now you have to start shopping? You're gonna miss the flight, man."

A petite, immaculately groomed black woman in her early twenties, Nadia looked like she was off on a weekend trip to Paris rather than visiting her mother in JA. She jutted out her jaw, indicating for Michael to take the credit card from her mouth.

"That plane ain't going nowhere without this gal. It can't, it's got my luggage on board. Hold these please." She deposited the clutch of new purchases in his arms, while taking the credit card and placing it back into her purse.

They said their goodbyes, ending in a long kiss. As she made her way through the passenger departure point, she stopped only to blow him a rather theatrical kiss; Michael was forced to smile. Nadia liked to be the centre of attention.

1

In her single breasted, grey wool suit with matching beret, she walked like a woman who knew she looked good and considered 'glamour' her middle name.

She worked on one of the Chanel counters at Harvey Nichols, and they'd met when he'd gone to purchase some scents for three other women. As soon as he saw her multiple reflections in the mirrors of the cosmetics hall, he knew he had to make some moves. When he was that determined, nothing could stop him. He got her to go through the entire range of products, even down to the bath oils, just to keep her chatting.

When it came to approaching women without it seeming like he was hitting on them, Michael was the Don. His whole working life had been spent in one sales job or another and he had perfected the gentle art of persuasion. Before he left Harvey Nichols with his Chanel purchases, he had secured her telephone number and was feeling confident that this was a 'result'. He told her the perfumes were a Christmas present for his mother. He felt slightly guilty about his lie, but he reasoned that all was fair in love and war. Who was it who said 'truth is the first casualty in love'?

They had met a few times over the Christmas period and it was clear they would become lovers. On the third date they succumbed to the inevitable and got 'down and nasty' on Michael's kitchen floor.

It was a relief that she was going to spend a month in JA, as she was getting a bit too attached for his liking. The interlude would put some space between them and would allow him the freedom to catch up on his 'runnings'.

At 29, he had no desire to settle down and he loved the chase as much now as he had ever done in his past. He loved women, it was as simple as that. To deny so many of them the pleasure of his company would be nothing short of selfish. Why be happy with one fish when there was such a big ocean out there? He had asked himself that question for as long as he could remember.

From the day he got his first hard-on as a boy, Michael

Hughes knew his passion in life. When other kids were collecting football stickers, he was stealing girlie mags from his local newsagents. By the age of thirteen, he had amassed a vast collection and earned a small fortune hiring them out to his classmates. He was tall for his age and this had proved a real asset when it came to removing the booty from the top shelves of shops.

At 6' 3" his height and well-toned body was as useful in the securing of female forms today as it had been in his childhood raids. This time the pleasures were definitely of a three dimensional kind.

He pressed the lift button and adjusted his tie looking at his reflection in the shiny steel lift doors. He checked the time again on his watch. Eleven twenty-four; the morning was over and he hadn't made any money yet. As he waited for the lift to arrive, he ran through in his mind the jobs he had to sort out for the day. Things were rough in the recession hit world of computer sales. Long gone were the boom days of the 80's when every Tom, Dick and Delbert was living large as a salesman. Today, he was working his butt off to make a sale that in the good times he wouldn't have to get out of bed for. But he consoled himself with the fact that it was the same for everyone and was grateful that, unlike scores of other computer businesses, he had not been visited by the receivers.

With his brother Joseph, he had started Mac In-Touch five years ago supplying new and secondhand Apple Macintosh computers to the booming publishing and graphic design market. In the good days, they had a big showroom on the Edgware Road and employed six members of staff, but as the recession started to bite business fell off dramatically. They had to move to smaller premises further up on the less salubrious Kilburn High Road and the staff had to go. Today, it was just Joseph, himself and the secretary, Cynthia that kept the business going.

He looked again at his watch. Eleven twenty-six. He would never be back at the office before noon as he had planned.

3

After what seemed an eternity, the lift arrived and the doors slid open. Among the crowded gaggle of Iranian travellers, she stood out a mile. About 36 years old, she was casually dressed in jeans and denim shirt with the arms of a cream aran jumper tied around her neck. Blonde with an attractive face, even with a little too much make-up, she had the look of someone who clearly had the confidence which comes with cash.

Michael wasn't that keen on blondes, but her eyes fixed so intently on his face and body, it was impossible not to notice her. He pressed the lift button to take him to Level 1 in the airport car park.

He felt her gaze piercing the side of his face. He looked at her again and briefly held her stare. It was the kind of stare that was hard to analyse. Her nose was pointing upwards and her nostrils slightly flared, yet her eyes were inviting. Her body language was confusing. Michael was intrigued, trying to work out if her manner was one of hostility or curiosity.

The lift doors opened and he stepped out onto the dirty concrete to find his silver BMW.

"Excuse me, would you mind helping me with this?"

He turned to check whether the request was directed at him. It was the blonde from the lift and he was the only person around. She had both hands round the handle of a large Louis Vitton suitcase and was attempting to lift it with obvious difficulty.

"I'm sorry to trouble you, but I didn't realise how heavy the case would be without a trolley. I hope you don't mind, you look pretty strong."

Her accent was clearly Sloanie and had that upper class arrogance that made the word 'sorry' sound anything but apologetic. There was no hint of a smile on her face and her request bordered on a command. *What is her story?* She was clearly confident by the direct nature of her speech.

As ever the charmer, Michael stepped to the woman's aid.

"No problem, my pleasure," he said with a polite smile.

4

From when he was no more than five years old, his grandfather had nicknamed him 'the charmer'. His grandfather used to joke that he would be "a devil with the women" when he got older, because he could "charm the birds in the trees." Michael learned early that a cute smile could get you a long way with women. When the ladies from his mother's church group would visit the family home, it was always 'lickle Mikey' they wanted to hug, because he had such a sweet smile.

He picked up the suitcase, overcompensating for its supposedly excessive weight . It jerked upwards with ease. To Michael's surprise it was extremely light and he wondered if she was making a joke at his expense.

She pointed to the left and informed him that she was parked several rows ahead. He followed her and was about to make a mindless comment on the mild January weather, when she beat him to it.

"You have very broad shoulders, is that natural or is it gym induced?"

Michael smiled, feeling slightly embarrassed at the cold, uncharming tone in the woman's voice.

"Well I like to keep myself in shape, so I do train every week. Healthy in mind and body, that's me. Do you work out?"

Her response was no response. She simply turned and looked at him with a blank expression, which confused him even more. He just couldn't work this woman out at all. Was she trying to be offensive? Was it a poor attempt at a come-on? Was she just one of those eccentric upper class women who are some unfathomable law unto themselves?

He was accustomed to the advances many white women, particularly middle class ones, made towards him. Being big built with strong features and a short goatee beard, Michael was 'fair game' for many white women. The personification of the black stud fantasy. He was well aware of it and used it when it suited him. On other occasions it pissed him off, especially when those women treated him like a fuck machine who could only function on a sexual level. Not

5

only that, but some of them tried to provoke him with insults to spur him into giving them rough sex. The way Michael saw it, their sexual fantasies were just that: theirs. He didn't need to hear any slackness in his ears to get him to give them the 'agony' they so desired. Call it political.

He considered making another attempt at conversation, but the white woman's vibe was too negative. He decided to see her to her car and get on his way.

They approached a muddy, green Range Rover parked with the rear of the vehicle close to a concrete wall. She walked to the back and opened the large tailgate. Michael followed her around the back, negotiating his way as precisely as possible, careful not to get mud on his dark blue Hugo Boss suit. He easily lifted the case into the boot and slammed the tailgate firmly. Before he could walk off, the woman furtively looked around the car park then stared hard at Michael.

"OK, we'll have to be quick." She spoke in hushed, breath-filled tones in contrast to her earlier cold and abrasive manner. With her stare still fixed on him, she undid the metal button of her jeans and started to unzip herself. Michael gulped. He had been party to all kinds of sexual advances in his time, but this one took him by surprise.

He put the palms of his hands up in a 'stop' sign.

"Whoa..! Cho' woman, is this some kind of a wind-up? You crazy or somet'ing?"

As always when he was getting annoyed, his 'queen's English', cultured salesman's voice took on a more streetlike intonation.

The woman ignored his protestations and began to unbutton her shirt from the bottom upwards, revealing the white flesh of her stomach.

"Look, you do want to fuck me, don't you? You think you're a bit of a lad don't you, well here's your chance to show me what you can do."

It was not an inquiry or a request, but a challenge. Her voice was low, but there was an aggressive and croaky edge to it. If Michael wasn't mistaken, she was getting turned on.

He hesitated for a moment, unsure whether he should take the bait or just turn his back and walk away. But it was too late for that and he knew it. The woman's right hand had disappeared into her white lacy panties as she started the job that she required this tall, athletic stranger to finish . She breathed heavily through a slightly opened mouth, as her excitement mounted. Michael's options diminished rapidly. He could feel himself being aroused with her every moan. He stepped towards her and pulled the panties down to her knees. The first thing he noticed was that she wasn't a natural blonde. About 5' 5", her toned petite body and well-shaped ass were indications that this was a woman who kept herself very much in shape. He held her by the waist and flipped her over like a doll, positioning her with her bottom towards him. The logistics were awkward, but not impossible. The Range Rover was parked too close to the concrete wall for him to take her from the concealed area behind the car. Instead, they moved to the back corner of the car, allowing her to hold onto the wall and the tailgate for support. While most of Michael and much of her body were concealed by the Rover, her hands and face were in view to any passing pedestrians.

But that didn't trouble them. Michael felt his heartbeat quicken as he clutched the inside of her thighs. The warmth of her flesh was a contrast to the cold winter air. The thrill of the unexpected nature of this public sexual encounter and the possibility of detection were exciting him. The thought of danger was one thing that always gave him a buzz. He was a risk taker and the thrill was as addictive as a drug. He unzipped his flies and struggled to get his swollen member out of his pants. His partner was getting impatient.

"Come on, what are you waiting for? I want you inside me. Now!"

He caressed the entrance to her sex gently with his left hand and grew stiffer as he felt just how much she wanted him inside of her. She was soaking. With his right hand he guided the head of his penis between her buttocks, lifting her clean off the floor.

Whether he liked it or not, Michael Hughes really was the true African stereotype. Nature had blessed him with a large sexual organ and many women were curious to sample just what he could do with such awesome apparatus. However, the constraining position of the woman's jeans was making entry somewhat problematic. Michael pulled the jeans down to her ankles with his foot, enabling her to open her legs wider and fully accommodate his manhood.

She let out a loud moan and then a gasp as he eased his erect penis into the tight, moist confines of her vagina. He pushed a little to allow his penis to disappear inside her. She gasped again, almost in shock at the depths he managed to reach within her. He withdrew slightly. The dark hue of his penis contrasted against the pale whiteness of her buttocks. He gripped her behind hard and slowly worked himself back inside her, the rhythm of his hips controlling proceedings. Then he pulled his cock as far back as he could, near the lips of her vagina, his shaft glistening with the moisture of her sex. Slowly, he pushed it back in teasingly, then pumped harder, her increasing wetness making a delicious squishing sound, as he moved in and out, as he thrust himself against her harder and faster.

The woman glanced back over her shoulder momentarily, a look of disbelief on her face. Her fingers gripped the concrete support with greater firmness, arching her back to take Michael's mass deep inside her. His movement became steadily faster and his mind more dizzy. He was fucking her like a man possessed. Her blonde hair swung wildly in front of him, her moans grew increasingly louder. She clearly wanted to be fucked. Plain and simple.

Her cries of ecstasy were now so loud that for a moment he thought about stopping. But Michael knew his dick well enough to know it wouldn't allow him to halt at this stage in the game. A Japanese family, pushing a trolley laden with luggage nearby, looked bemused in the direction of the loud orgasmic groans then realised simultaneously the reason for the disturbance. The young boy smiled and attempted to peer underneath the the Range Rover, but his father ranting in Japanese, swiftly grabbed him and hurried his family away from the scene.

Michael and blondie were too far gone to notice or care about any interruption. His head lightened as he felt a surge. Her time was up. He pulled his wood from her with expert timing and shivered.

Michael closed his eyes and leaned with his back against the Rover's tailgate, tucking himself in, searching for breath and trying to make sense of it all. His recovery was cut short by the slam of a car door and the roar of an engine. He straightened just as the Range Rover pulled out of the parking space and headed down the exit ramp. Michael kissed his teeth irritably and wondered who was more crazy, 'that bitch' or him for giving her the pleasure of his wood. At the rear doors of a Transit van, a small group of white working class lads wearing Spanish sombreros, shorts and T shirts, cheered and applauded as Michael turned and walked to his BM. Adjusting his tie sheepishly, he returned their appreciation of his performance with a thumbs up and a chuckle.

As he sped down the M4 into central London, Michael noticed the dry mud on his suit. He cursed and looked at the clock on the dashboard. Eleven forty-eight. He was going to be late. He dialled the office on his mobile and asked Cynthia to reschedule his appointments for the day. He now regretted wasting time with the crazy white woman. 'Time is money' he was always saying and here he was wasting valuable money-earning time on some ungrateful, stuck-up, crazy bitch. His brother was always fretting about the business and Michael pictured him having a seizure if he knew what he had been up to.

He loved Joseph, or 'Josey' as the family called him, but the two of them were as different as brothers could be. Josey was three years older but to Michael it might as well have been ten. Josey was married at 23 to Diane who he met at college, and was very much the family man with two kids and a nice three-bedroomed semi up in Woodford Green. Michael on the other hand, saw marriage like filling in a tax return form. It was something you had to do, but if you could put off doing it for as long as possible, so much the better.

Josey took on a lot of responsibility early and felt it was way past time that his younger brother started taking life a lot more seriously and "focused" himself.

He could not understand how Michael could "waste so much energy" chasing women and not realise how it diminished his potential to make the business a success. Michael remembered only too well the incident a few years earlier when he had five grand's worth of Apple Mac Quadra machines stolen from the boot of his car. It was parked up outside a girl's house one afternoon when he should have been delivering them to a customer. Michael was too engrossed in his 'Close Encounters of the Only Kind' to hear the alarm go off, as a couple of youngsters crowbarred open the boot and legged it with the gear. The equipment wasn't insured and Josey had to be physically restrained when his brother broke the news of what had happened.

In the blazing row that followed, Josey reckoned that his brother's dick was responsible for "90 per cent of the problems in the black community today." Michael tried to argue a bit of political history and state that his love of sex was due to slavery and the deliberate breakdown of the family structure. But it was harder to convince his brother that that was why they were five grand out of pocket. Slavery was one thing, stupidity another.

While they were poles apart in personality, they were nevertheless family and if nothing else, you have to accept your family for what they are. Also, both brothers knew that the business needed their different styles. Josey was a careful methodical planner who ran things efficiently. He was the one with an HND in electronic engineering and provided the technical dimension to the business. Michael on the other hand took care of the marketing and sales side of things. His boundless energy and confidence helped to win new business and clients. Had it not been for Michael, Mac In-Touch would never have happened. It was while Joseph was an engineer working at Apple Mac's UK head office that his brother, who was working in computer sales, suggested that they set up the company.

As he parked up the BMW on the yellow lines outside the shop on Kilburn High Road, he saw the woman traffic warden moving in like a bee to honey. Michael rushed towards her with a big smile on his face and his hands together in a prayer-like position.

"Please, please, please ," he pleaded in an exaggerated voice. "My mother is sick in hospital and she asked me to get her a computer so she can type a will on her death bed." He took the traffic warden's hand and kissed it. Her resolve weakened. Her features began to soften, as her tough middle-aged face slowly broke into a smile.

"Go on. I'll be back in fifteen minutes," she said, putting her computerised keypad back into her bag.

Michael thanked her and walked briskly into the Mac In-Touch shop.

Sandwiched between a stationery shop and an insurance brokers, Mac In-Touch's small glass frontage was crammed with second-hand computer equipment 'on sale'. The store stood out due to the string of flashing coloured lights running around the inside frame of the window. Tacky, Michael had always thought, but effective.

Inside, the small shop housed shelves of computers, printers, accessories and software boxes. Cynthia was busily typing on a keyboard. A petite girl with big eyes and big gold earrings, she sported a short, ragga-style hair cut. Not long out of college, she had worked at Mac In-Touch for only three months, but in that time she had proved herself a useful asset due to her hard-working nature and common sense. Her girlish face was deceptive. Cynthia could lash out a barrage of abuse which even surprised worldly-wise Michael. She was confident and bright, however, apt to speaking her mind which was often the last thing the brothers wanted to hear.

As Michael entered, Cynthia looked him up and down with a shocked expression on her face.

"Lawd have mercy. T'ings so bad that you haffe go sleep rough, Michael?"

He'd forgotten about the state of his suit and he quickly tried to brush the mud from his jacket.

"Yeah. I fell over at the airport."

She looked him straight in the eye. "Yes Michael, but who was the woman who fell on top of you?"

"You're funny Cynthia. You jus' jealous it wasn't you."

She kissed her teeth and smiled. "Yeah Michael, right. I have no interest in joining your roll call of pubic appearances, thank you very much. I'll leave that privilege for the women out there who don't know what you're about."

"Do you know what I'm about?"

"I know enough to realise that one of these days you're gonna get burned," Cynthia said.

TWO

A bead of sweat trickled down the ridges of his abdomen and rested in his navel. In the mirrored doors of the fitted wardrobe, he looked at the flexing biceps in his right arm and tasted the sweat pouring down his face. He let out a grunt. That was enough for today. He carefully lay the heavy dumbbell down on the rubber mat between his feet and stood up from the exercise bench.

Mopping the sweat from his firm torso with a towel, he walked to the small bedside table where his large glass of orange juice waited to reward him for a completed workout.

This was Michael's early morning ritual, a vigorous thirty minute bout of exercise using a set of dumbbells before facing the frustrating hour and twenty minute drive from Blackheath to Kilburn. The exercise set him up for the day and rid him of any lingering stress that a night's sleep had not relieved. He liked to keep his body in shape not only because it made him feel good, but because women appreciated a man who had a defined body and looked after himself. In the perpetual quest for women, every available weapon in the armoury had to be used. Gone were the days when a man could look like Wurzel Gumage and still expect to pull some attractive woman. The black women he was interested in wanted a man who had it all, and they were within their rights to demand it.

Michael was the first to admit that he had a big ego, but he reckoned his charm tempered that trait. Not only did he have the physique, he also had the finesse, lyrics and lifestyle that turned a lot of women on, but he knew the dangers too. A woman can spot arrogance at four hundred paces; if a guy thinks he's 'got it going on' and shows it, she isn't going to give you the time of day. There was an art involved and you had to get the balance just right.

After a refreshing shower and the usual grooming routine, his stomach began to speak to him. Over a breakfast of cereal, kiwis, banana and papaya, he skimmed through a copy of the previous day's Financial Times, which he had not yet found time to read. The winter morning sun beamed across the pages. The stories were mostly about multi-million pound takeover bids of large companies. It all seemed financial light years away from the turnover of his own business. But as he liked to tell his brother, "Don't just think big, think massive." At the moment things were tight financially, but he was confident that the economy would soon pick up. 'It had better' he thought, because he was running close to the wind these days. He struggled each month to meet the payments on the three-bedroomed house and he was overdue in paying the finance people for his year old, 3 Series BMW. The house was probably a bit of an extravagance especially as he was rarely in, but he'd bought it at the height of the property boom and it was now worth less than he had paid for it. He was staring at a fifteen grand loss if he tried to sell it. Come to think of it, the car was also an extravagance, but he reasoned that he needed it for work and it wouldn't do the image of the company any good to be seen running around in some old, clapped-out Cortina.

He had tried to cut down on his outgoings. He had even considered going easy on the wining and dining of women, but there again, all work and no play made Jack a dull boy. What he needed was to start dating black women with serious money. That type of woman seemed a bit thin on the ground these days. They were either already taken, or had an 'attitude'. He had dated a string of buppy women and wannabes in the past and sometimes they seemed more trouble than they were worth. Too many of them were obsessed with trying to be better than their black man instead of trying to progress with him. He had no problems with women getting ahead in their careers but it didn't mean you had to step on the black man to get there.

He lay down the newspaper and looked at the unopened bills that had arrived that morning. He threw them down on the pine table. Cho'! They could wait. Picking up his jacket he headed down the stairs which led to the hall and study, pausing briefly to adjust a crooked mahogany framed print of an African village scene on the wall. He was proud of his home and liked to keep it looking good. It was one of six recently built, detached three-storey houses on Blackheath's Old Dover Road. On the ground floor, the front door opened into a spacious hall which in turn led to a study with French windows opening onto a small, but beautifully landscaped, garden. Up the arched staircase, the second floor housed the lounge, kitchen diner and bathroom. Finally, the top floor had one master bedroom and two smaller ones. The whole place had natural beech flooring and the walls were painted ivory. Artifacts and furniture from Africa, India and Indonesia gave the house an exotic sophistication. He used to go for the matt black, hi-tech, bachelor look, but decided over a year ago that it was time for a change. Too many of his male friends had pads like that and it had become a cliché. An interior designer friend, Lucy, worked to his rough brief and had done the job just right. It made sense to get a woman to design the interior, because he wanted it to appeal to women. And it seemed to work. Without exception, every woman he had invited back to his yard had fallen in love with the place. If anything Lucy had done her job too well. It was often difficult to get some of the women to leave.

Once downstairs, Michael slipped on his jacket. A loud knocking at the front door stopped him in his tracks. The violent nature of the knock made him suspicious. He stepped to one side slowly and concealed himself among the coats hanging on the hat stand in the hall. Through the frosted glass panels of the front door, he could make out the silhouettes of two burly-looking men. No one except the postman ever knocked his door in the morning and the post had already been delivered.

"I'm sure he's fucking well in there," he heard one of callers say.

The door was knocked with even more aggression. From his hiding place Michael saw the letterbox flap rise and a pair of eyes peer into the hallway. He quickly retracted his head back behind the stand.

"Let's wait for a while out here. He's probably in the

shower."

The flap was lowered but Michael could still hear the men in conversation outside his front door. He didn't recognise the cockney accents and didn't fancy making their acquaintances. The memory of the time he had been wakened early one Sunday by the sound of someone kicking down his front door flashed through his mind. It had turned out to be the boyfriend of the girl lying in his arms. It ended with an undignified punch-up in the street outside. Although Michael was a lot bigger than the boyfriend, the guy was driven by such a rage that he refused to take his blows and call it a day. In the meantime, an amused crowd of neighbours had revelled in the spectacle until someone decided to call the police. To add further embarrassment, he was arrested still wearing only his boxer shorts and spent two hours in a cell at Blackheath police station before being released without charge. His humiliation continued on the long walk home from the station. The sight of a grown man walking the streets, dressed only in his boxer shorts, was still worth a good laugh in south-east London and a group of youths chased him part of the way, enjoying every minute of it. The situation could not get any worse, right? Wrong. To add insult to injury the girl had left by the time he'd got back, thus locking him out of his own house.

Thinking about it now, he was determined to avoid that kind of foolishness at any cost. This time there were two of them. He looked at his watch. Eight nineteen. He didn't have time to work out who the men were and the reason for the early morning visit. Carefully, he opened the study door and crept into the room. He closed the door gently and hastened to the French windows where he made good his exit. By the side of each house was a small walkway leading to a tall wooden gate. Throwing himself high in the air, he gripped onto the top of the wooden fence separating the neighbour's garden from his and scrambled over, landing softly in the muddy flowerbed on the other side. He cursed as his newly-polished, black Italian brogues buried themselves in the clay soil. He quickly crossed his neighbour's lawn, wiping his muddy shoes in the grass as he went. He tackled the fence on the other side more carefully. This time he landed firmly on the concrete paving in the next garden, but a sickening ripping sound made him grimace with complete dread. He turned to see a six inch long strip of black Armani wool suit, hanging from a protruding nail in the fence. He shut his eyes tight and opened them again slowly. The tear didn't disappear. His favourite suit was ruined. He kicked the fence in frustration and cursed. As he made his way solemnly towards the wooden gate, he noticed a woman standing looking through the French windows of the house, mouth wide open in amazement. Did villains wear Italian suits on burglaries nowadays? Michael smiled, nodded and gave her a thumbs up sign.

He peered out cautiously from behind the neighbour's wooden gate. The two men were still hanging around outside his front door. Fortunately, their attention was focused on his house so neither of them noticed Michael as he walked towards his BMW parked some way down the road. For once, he was grateful that all the immediate parking spaces had been taken when he arrived home late the previous night.

From the harassed look on her boss' face, Cynthia decided that this was perhaps not a good time to jest about his appearance. She simply shook her head. Michael grunted a greeting to her and went to clean up in the toilet. He emerged several minutes later with few visible clues as to his morning's ordeal.

In the back office, Josey was carefully replacing a micro chip on a circuit board when his brother popped in. They exchanged pleasantries.

"What's up, Mikey? You look under pressure, man." Josey was concerned but tried to make the remark sound jovial.

He knew his brother well enough to know when the boy was distressed.

Michael smiled and rubbed his neatly trimmed goatee.

"Oh you know how t'ings stay. Sometimes you get up and life jus' waan lick you down again."

His remark was cryptic enough for Josey to figure that his brother wasn't going to share his troubles with him.

Brothers they may have been, but the physical similarities between Josey and Michael were slight. They had the same dark, ebony skin, but Josey was a good four inches shorter than his brother and whereas Michael had a Dick Tracey square jaw line, Josey had a rounder, gentler face. Josey's encroaching middle-age spread was a sign that he wallowed in the comforts of homely life. Josey looked like the sort of man who wore woollen slippers and enjoyed settling down in front of the television with the warmth of his family surrounding him. He seemed relaxed with life and at times Michael envied his brother's mellow mind. But while he admired and respected his brother, he knew he couldn't be like him, well not for a good while anyway. There was too much fun out there. He loved life in the fast lane too much and wasn't ready for a gentle cruise down the leafy country lanes of life.

"Listen Mikey, me and Diane are cooking up a big yard style lunch, a week on Sunday. It's her birthday so can you make sure you're available?"

Michael laughed.

"What's this 'me and Diane' bit? Since when you turned chef, Josey? The last time you tried to cook you nearly burned the house down!"

"Well lickle brother, the proof of the pudding is in the eating. Just fetch yahself up to Woodford next weekend and then come talk to me about 'catch a fire.' And Michael, bring some nice respectable woman with you this time. No lickle dibbi dibbi jail bait like you bring to the Christmas party."

Michael laughed with mock indignation.

"What do you mean jail bait? That girl was seventeen. And mature for her age, too. How was I to know she was just a teenager? She told me she was twenty-four."

Josey shook his head. He'd long stopped trying to keep his brother on the straight and narrow when it came to women.

"Listen, Diane wasn't too happy about it you know. Bianca will be seventeen before long and I'd be vexed to think of her going with someone like you when she was that young."

Bianca was Josey's ten-year-old daughter. It was a little too near the knuckle for Michael's liking. Michael squinted with indignation at what his brother was suggesting.

"Hey, listen, if I'd known she was so young I'd have walked a mile. When I found out, I stopped it dead. I ain't no cradle snatcher. So don't lay no heavy guilt trip on me, Josey. I ain't the one, bro."

"Okay, okay, I'm sorry, but make sure you listen and hear what I'm saying. Come on, man , we've got work to sort out."

Josey decided it was better to deal with the immediate business needs, as the mood was getting a little too heated. They sat and discussed the plans for the week and what jobs needed doing. Josey mentioned that a contact at Apple Mac UK had told him about a visiting delegation of Russian businessmen who were visiting Britain that week to check out sources of Apple Mac computers for the Eastern Bloc market. They had contacted Apple Mac UK, but as they were only interested in second-hand machines, the parent company had been of little use. However, Josey's contact had mentioned Mac In-Touch to them and they were most interested. They were only over for one day, stopping the night then flying back the next morning.

Michael's eyes lit up.

"Rewind selector, rewind. Yah say they're here fe only one day?"

"Yeah. They arrive at Heathrow on Friday at 9.00am. But they are being met by a guy from Micro Chippie who is taking them to see their operation before they come here in the afternoon."

Michael kissed his teeth. This was a big opportunity for them to make some serious dollars. It was good news that the Russians were coming, but bad news that they would be going to Micro Chippie first. The old Eastern Bloc was a booming market for computer hardware and Apple Macs were now more desirable than Levis and Beatles records over there. Such was the demand for Apple Macs in the former Soviet Union, that a multi-million pound trade in stolen computers had developed between British villains and the Russian mafia. Across London, Apple Macs were being stolen with frightening regularity. There had been a number of attempted break-ins at Mac In-Touch, but the Fort Knox-style security and expensive alarm system wired to the local police station, had so far managed to repel all would-be burglars. The word on the internet was that Micro Chippie had a dubious back door trade in stolen Macs which they moved to other UK cities. If that was the case, Mac In-Touch couldn't compete on fair terms with Micro Chippie when it came to trading with the Russians. There was no way they could sell legitimate computers for less than the price of stolen ones.

Michael kissed his teeth again. He looked at his brother and shook his head slowly.

"Dis cyaan work, star. It cyaan work! Seriously Josey, we've got to sort something out or we ain't gonna get jack shit out of this one. You know what I mean?"

Josey was in agreement. But what could they do?

"Lemme think on this one bro. There has to be an answer." There was a determination in Michael's face which pleased his brother.

"I ain't seen you so excited about business in a long time. If you can come up with a solution, I'm all ears."

THREE

They say that like buses, trouble comes in threes and this week trouble seemed to to have Michael Hughes' name all over it. He'd been making his way home, fighting the bumper to bumper traffic down the Edgware Road when his mobile rang.

"Hello Jackie, long time… What'ya mean you're in trouble…? Yeah, yeah but what sort of trouble…? But why can't you just say on the phone…? Okay, okay stop crying, calm down. Yeah, it's no problem. I'll meet you. Look, everything's gonna be fine. Just calm down. Yeah, I can meet you… I'll see you at Bar Royale in Camden in about an hour's time. Don't worry, everything will be fine."

He snapped the phone shut and tried running through all the possibilities in his mind. What was up with Jackie? He started with pregnancy, but quickly dismissed that one. He'd been too careful. Maybe it was just family problems, or work worries. Had she been fired? Yeah that was it, he figured. But didn't she say it was women's problems? Men got fired too. It couldn't be that. She couldn't have some sort of disease, could she? He ran through all the permutations in his head, but he was still left wondering.

His mind flashed back to the time he'd first met Jackie at a sales conference at the Prince Albert Hotel in Victoria nearly six years ago. She had been in another division of the telecommunications company he worked for, selling pagers. They got chatting in the hotel bar after dinner and as the evening wore on they got more and more merry. She was a real laugh-a-minute kind of woman. A neat, curvaceous woman, with wide eyes and a cheeky smile. She was twenty-three when he first met her, although her spirit was that of a much older woman. He had had some weed with him, which he had brought along for when the lectures got boring, so he could sneak out and get charged in the Gents. He suggested to Jackie that they could avail themselves of the relaxing qualities of the 'erb in her hotel room. The kind offer was graciously accepted.

The telecommunications company had taken great care to make sure that their sales employees would have a pleasant two days at the sales conference. The Prince Albert Hotel had been recently refurbished in grand Victorian style. The rooms came equipped with four poster beds and were decked out in lavish reproduction carpentry. The ensuite bathroom, with its dark mahogany wood fittings and shiny brass taps were typical of the hotel's attention to detail.

In her room, Michael kicked off his shoes and lay on the sumptuous bed, building up a large spliff. Meanwhile, Jackie was busy pouring brandy into two glasses on the small wooden cabinet bar. As she'd bent down to open the cabinet door, Michael couldn't help but notice the ample proportions of her bottom, tightly contained in a black skirt. He smiled to himself. He liked a girl with a big behind. Although a slim 5' 3", Jackie had a bottom that looked as if it begged to be clasped in a man's hands.

Michael lay spreadeagled on the bed and pulled on the spliff with a look of relaxation on his face. The vibes were level and definitely mellow. Jackie took the spliff and sat at the end of the bed smiling. She noticed the contented look on his face.

"You look like a cat who's just had the cream."

"Jackie, you know you're right. I do feel like a lickle pussy right now."

She threw a cushion at him and pretended to be offended.

"You're disgusting, you know. You're a rude man."

It was Michael's turn to feign innocence.

"What d'you mean, Jackie? I just said a felt like a little pussy cat to get all warm and cosy with."

She laughed and threw another cushion at him.

Laying back on the soft folds of the bed, looking up towards the ceiling, they let the weed lift them. The spliff was first rate sensi and within a short time they both felt well charged. The mood was one of total relaxation. Michael got up to dim the lights while Jackie programmed some mellow soul sounds on the room's hi-fi system, then she made her way over to the bathroom. The sound of a shower head gushing with water was like music to Michael's ears and the sight of steam wafting out through the slightly ajar bathroom door was an invitation he couldn't resist. He pulled himself off the bed and went to join her, following the trail of Jackie's clothes on the carpet, into the bathroom. He wasn't sure what reaction he'd get, but his head was buzzing too much to give it a lot of thought. The naked silhouette behind the frosted glass was on his mind. That they were going to be sleeping together that night was a certainty, but he was aware that he might still have to go through the usual rituals before getting down to it.

In Michael's experience, everybody played games, but women had a very specific kind of game to play. It was all about preserving an image of virtue. It seemed that no matter how liberated and confident the woman, there was always this in-built fear of being viewed as a slut. As a result, they often had a slight resistance to the strong come-on and would hold back just enough to make it clear that sex wasn't entirely what they were about.

Jackie was too independent and determined a woman to have time for games. Michael removed his shirt and trousers and folded them neatly on the brass towel rail behind him. As he opened the warm shower door, she smiled invitingly and began rubbing the soapy lather over her small but pert breasts in a deliberate manner.

Michael wasted no time in joining her. With his eyes closed he ducked under the jet of water. The powerful blast from the shower felt hot and invigorating on his naked flesh. Moving downward from his neck, Jackie worked the soap into a creamy lather and massaged it into his firm dark flesh. The white foam flowed down his torso, following the contours of his form, sliding down his pelvis and between his thighs. He leant back against the tiled wall for support as her fingers circled his nipples, teasing them into a state of erection. Then she massaged his back and shoulders with her comforting fingers. She worked her way downwards, to

23

the base of his spine then over his buttocks, separating the cheeks gently and giving them a little tweak, before her hand disappeared underneath. He felt her hand as it cupped his balls gently from behind, then softly teased them between her fingers. She could feel his penis slowly rise. Crouching as she moved lower, water cascading down her back, the stiffness of his organ turned her on.

She worked up a lather and smoothed it into his pubic hairs and around his balls and crotch as water splashed all around. Breathing heavily, Michael pulled her up towards him and caressed her breasts, bringing his finger down from her collar bone to her nipple. He toyed with her nipples, rubbing them up and down with his palms. Occasionally, she would slide a soapy hand between his legs and gently massage between his buttocks, drawing her fingernails over his tight ass as the hot blast of water gushed over their bodies. It felt good. Michael's head buzzed wildly. The combination of sensi, alcohol and the hot, steamy cubicle made his mind feel light and detached from his body. He let out a deep gasp of air as he felt the warmth of her mouth on the head of his penis. Slowly pulling back his foreskin, she gently ran her mouth along the length of his shaft with the roof of her mouth stroking the tip of its head. As her tongue danced expertly around his penis, shivers of ecstasy ran up his spine. The bubbling excitement made his knees quiver almost uncontrollably and for a moment he worried that he might lose his balance. *This woman certainly knows how to give head*, he thought with a sigh of pleasure.

Jackie sensed his unsteadiness and slowed the proceedings down. She turned off the shower and allowed her eyes to peruse his body as the last drops of water trickled down to his feet. She was clearly impressed. She pulled a large fluffy towel from the rail and, with circling strokes, began to dry his chest, then his back, buttocks and legs. That kind of pampering was just what the doctor ordered and made a pleasant change for Michael. He normally had to do all the coaxing and caressing. Tonight, Jackie wanted to call the shots and he was more than happy for that to happen, especially as his head seemed to be floating a foot above his neck.

She took him by the hand and led him into the bedroom where he slumped, stomach down, onto the bed. He felt blissfully at ease.

"You've got a cute bottom Michael, do you know that?" Jackie stood at the foot of the bed admiring him.

He mumbled something she couldn't hear in reply. He was concentrating on the movements of her hands which were now on the back of his ankles, pulling his legs apart. He wasn't sure what she was doing, but was happy to go along for the ride. He'd already decided that whatever this woman wanted she'd get. Suddenly, he felt a hot gust of air on his flesh, then her teeth biting his buttocks. It started gently, but as she got aroused, the biting became more vigorous and frenzied. Michael gritted his teeth, but it was pleasurable. He had slipped into an erotic trance and no amount of pain would shake him out of it.

Jackie didn't ease up. She gripped his buttocks harder and pulled them apart before the tip of her tongue made slow circle strokes around the centre of his anus. His buttocks quickly tightened, then gradually began to relax and soften. It was a new sensation for him, but it felt good, embarrassingly good. The stimulation flowed from his ass underneath his crotch, until it reached the tip of his penis. Slowly, as the pleasure crept over him, he relaxed and let her tongue do its work. Her frantic panting was proof enough that she was getting off doing it, and if she was enjoying it, so was he.

She soon switched her attention to other areas of his body. She rolled him over onto his back and he was only too happy to oblige. Then she disappeared to the bathroom and returned promptly with two belts from the cotton bathrobes provided by the Hotel. Without saying a word, she pulled his hand towards one of the bedposts and proceeded to tie his wrist to the post. Michael saw what was coming, and her dominance turned him on; he certainly wasn't going to stop her now. She repeated the process with his left wrist before straddling his chest.

He briefly opened his eyes and looked straight in her horny eyes and whispered. "Jackie, you're one rude girl."

She grinned a cheeky grin and tilted her head slightly to accept the accolade. He felt the wetness from her pussy on his chest and it was driving his cock mad. He was totally in her hands and the thought excited him. It crossed his mind that he hardly knew this woman, yet they were playing some seriously deep sexual games. Thinking about it was a wicked turn-on.

Still astride him, she eased her way up his chest until her pussy was no more than a couple of inches away from his mouth. He stuck his tongue out to lick her wetness, but she drew it back.

"Uuh-unh! Wait for it. I'll tell you when."

The more she teased him, the more he wanted to taste her. His legs thrashed with impatience, but it did him no good. Jackie simply lowered herself down on him. She moved her pussy delicately along his face, allowing it to caress his nose before coming to rest on his mouth. *At last!* Michael salivated. His tongue darted into her vagina, gently playing with her clitoris, which throbbed with the pleasure of dominance. With the care of a true maestro he gently sucked her clitoris. She rocked backwards and forwards, pressing her pussy hard onto his mouth and let out a loud guttural moan. That was merely the beginning. Her rocking became swifter and wilder and the moaning became an intense, high-pitched howl. Gripping his arms for support, she raised herself up, unable to take any more. A strong orgasmic rush filled her head. She let out a loud, victorious shout and climaxed over his mouth.

After what seemed only a brief moment to Michael, her warm hand was enveloping his cock and vigorously caressing the shaft of his prick. He felt that familiar throbbing in his balls. His pelvis jerked once, twice, three times, then he let out a deep moan as he climaxed.

Since that first night at the hotel, he had been seeing Jackie on and off, and they had enjoyed many wild sexual experiences together. He had learned more about sex from that woman than anyone he'd slept with before. Even now, he could think of no one who had the same degree of sexual liberation as Jackie. She was a woman who didn't need sexual fantasies, because she preferred acting out whatever she wanted to experience sexually.

Jackie was an interesting sexual persona. It was she who had showed him that his buttocks and anus were erogenous zones. Until meeting her he'd associated the ass with 'batty men'. She made him admit that it was his own fear of homosexuality that had stopped him from exploring that area of his body. While she was unusual in being so up front, Michael had noticed of recent that the black women he was meeting were becoming more open on such sexual matters. He hadn't forgotten that only a few years earlier, most sisters refused to be down with oral sex. Undaunted, Michael nevertheless perfected his craft and soon had a tongue to match his wood. He was hot property in those days, because for many black women sex with him was their first taste of some serious 'downtown business'. Michael often claimed, without modesty or embarrassment, that his tongue had turned half the black women in south London on to cunnilingus. Like that Marcia in Crystal Palace who, once she had had her pussy properly administered in the oral sense, loved it so much she no longer wanted intercourse.

His oral fixation wasn't shared by his male acquaintances who often accused him of being 'nasty'. Michael would simply laugh at their criticisms and tell them, "It's probably your woman's pussy I'm servicing at the moment!"

Michael's mind drifted back to the Edgware Road and the traffic ahead. He looked at his Rolex and calculated the time it would take from his next stop to Camden. The slow moving traffic meant it took another ten minutes before he pulled up outside the computer accessory shop. He switched on the car alarm and moved quickly into the shop.

A moustached Asian man with thinning hair was behind the counter, staring perplexed at a computer screen. He looked up and smiled.

"Okay, boss. How are things?"

Michael shook hands with the man and exchanged greetings.

"Ahmed, you got the stuff?"

Ahmed confirmed the request with a nod and handed him a computer keyboard wrapped in clear bubblewrap polythene.

"It took me ages to find one of these. What do you need it for?"

"It would take too long to explain, Ahmed. What's the damage?"

They haggled for a moment about the price before Michael handed him the cash. The price was a little over the odds but this keyboard was going to be worth every penny and then some.

Michael arrived at Bar Royale bang on eight o'clock and sauntering through the door, was surprised to see Jackie already there, sitting at one of the stools at the bar. The bar was full of its usual young Camden club hipsters, both black and white. Michael couldn't help feeling that maybe his suit and tie were a little out of place and wondered why he had chosen to meet her there. With its loud music, Bar Royale was hardly the place for a quiet discussion.

Michael pushed his way to the bar where he gave a nod to a group of black youths at a table in the corner. "Yeah, safe," replied one in a wool Stussy hat. Michael turned to Jackie and put his arm around her, kissing her lightly on the cheek. He soon caught the barmaid's eye and ordered a Southern Comfort and ice for her while he held a Beck's.

Jackie looked a mess. Her lifeless hair was drawn back in

a small scrunchie, and her face looked pale. Her eyes looked worried. He didn't have to wait long to find out why.

"I think I'm pregnant and I'm going to keep it if I am. And yes, you're the father."

The directness of the statement caught him off guard and the swig of beer he'd just filled his mouth with, spurted out in a spray across the bar, followed by a coughing fit as he tried to clear his windpipe of residue Beck's. Jackie leapt to his aid and slapped his back hard to relieve the choking. After a minute, Michael regained his composure.

"Whoa, Jackie!" he said, still hoarse. "Just slow it down a bit, and start from the beginning. I mean, how? When? What? Who?"

Jackie gave an exaggerated sigh and looked at him.

"Michael, I'm sure a man of your age and experience must be able to answer the 'how' question. I've told you the 'who' and 'what'. I think you might be able to have a guess at the 'when'."

He had a worried expression on his face.

"But we used a condom? I remember. We used a condom. I don't remember which make, but I remember we used one. A rubber one."

"Don't be so sarcastic Michael. If your memory is so good you'll also remember that it came off when you pulled out."

She was tense and even with the loud rap music playing found it hard to disguise her irritation. The barmaid looked across as she mopped the spilt beer off the bar top with a cloth. She caught Michael's angry glare and quickly averted her eyes back to the bar.

"Maybe this isn't the best place to have a conversation like this, Jackie. Can we go for a drive?"

She agreed. They left their half-empty glasses and headed out into the chilly January evening. They climbed into his BMW and drove the short distance to Regent's Park where they sat in the car and talked for nearly two hours.

Jackie's period was three weeks overdue, but she hadn't gone to the doctor or taken a pregnancy test. She said she was too frightened to deal with the truth at the moment, a logic that Michael found hard to fathom. He felt slightly more relieved now. From the way she'd broken the news at the bar, it had sounded as if she was definitely pregnant. He was a gambling man and now that he had all the facts, he figured there was a good chance that she wasn't, even if his confidence ebbed a little when she explained that she'd never been late before. As his spar Alex was fond of saying, 'It nuh done till the big mampie sing'.

He drove her back to her flat in Stoke Newington in contemplative mood, before heading home himself. His business concerns and the prospect of the Russians coming at the end of the week were now far back in his mind. All he could think about was fatherhood. Maybe the pressure was getting to him after all.

He'd avoided being a baby father this long and the prospect of fatherhood at this moment in time wasn't one he relished. He had to agree with his brother that it was a 'miracle' that he'd 'not already fathered ten pickney, let alone one'. Michael was happy to carry on believing in miracles.

Okay, there had been a couple of close shaves which ended in abortions, but that was a while ago. Since then he had avoided the possibility of surprise packages by making sure his parcel was always properly wrapped but, as he discovered, sometimes the parcel can get damaged in the post. This was not good news. If the worse did come to the worse, he knew he wasn't ready for fatherhood, he just wasn't ready.

The thought of babies reminded him that he'd promised to drop round on a friend he'd not seen for a while who had recently become a mother. The car's clock flashed 10.28. He pulled out his mobile and dialled Angela's number.

Michael arrived at the terraced house in east London's Forest Gate area twenty minutes later. As she'd said, the key to the front door was under the mat in the porch.

The house, which smelt of cooking and nappies, was dark apart from a dim light upstairs.

"Is that you Michael?" a voice called from the bathroom as he closed the front door behind him.

"No, it's the big bad wolf."

"Come right up. You're good at feeling your way in the dark, aren't you?"

Angela was lying in a candle-illuminated bubble bath, soaping her thigh with a flannel. Michael greeted her with a peck on the cheek, before setting himself down on the closed toilet seat and asking her what was news. For once, Angela explained, she had managed to put the baby to sleep and had enough time to treat herself to a relaxing soak in the bath.

Angela used to work for a travel agency in the West End until three months ago, when she became a mum for the second time. Fortunately, Angela's mother was taking care of her eight year old granddaughter, Shanice, while the new mum got back on her feet.

Even submerged in soapy water, Angela was large, but had the stature to carry it gracefully. Her dark-skinned form peeked through the white bubbles and her large breasts bobbed up and down as she chatted eagerly about what she'd been doing in the last eighteen months. It had been that long since they'd seen each other.

Just over a year ago, she'd met a reggae producer who she had fallen madly in love with. But when she got pregnant he fled to New York and she had not heard from him since. Michael sympathised and thanked the gods that he wasn't the type of guy that would do that kind of thing. She intended to deal with the situation nevertheless, she told him. She wasn't the first woman to be deserted and all the others seemed to be coping.

Angela had a heart of gold and would help anyone in distress, but at the end of the day she wasn't a classic beauty. Even though in the past he had helped service her sexual needs from time to time, she was not the sort of girl Michael wanted on his arm when he went out raving. The women he took to clubs like Moonlighting had to be criss. He felt guilty about feeling that way, but he was a man and that was all there was to it. He'd even argued about it with one woman who wanted to know why, if a woman was good enough to sleep with, you wouldn't want to introduce her to your friends or family. It was hard to explain that to a woman, but other men knew the lick. That was his answer. She didn't accept it and hurled a stream of abuse at him containing words like 'two-faced' and 'dog'.

"They're huge aren't they?" Angela grinned. She had noticed how Michael's eyes kept looking at her large swollen breasts surfacing on top of the bubbles in the bath.

"You took the words right out of my mouth," he sang with a mischievous grin.

He'd really only come round for a chat, but as he now sat naked on the sofa with her face between his legs, he wasn't going to complain. Angela was doing a fine job.

She stood up to sit next to him and brought one of her heavy breasts out of her satin night shirt. Michael squeezed the large erect nipple and was rewarded with a small white jet of milk, which spurted onto his stomach. For some reason he found it funny and giggled.

Angela confessed that it had been a long time since she'd had sex and the frenzied way in which she unfolded the condom onto his dick, seemed to bear this out. She quickly mounted his cock and was soon working it hard. Michael held her ass tight and pulled her down hard. He placed his mouth over her nipples and began to tease them with his tongue, then he began to suck and was soon tasting her sweet milk. It wasn't long before Angela climaxed and Michael's white fluid entered her. A kind of cycle was completed.

FOUR

He just couldn't work out why the fault was occurring. Every time he pressed the 'Print' command key, a warning popped up on the computer screen with the words "Resource not found." He checked the cable connections again and the software, but it still wasn't happening. He'd tried phoning Josey for some advice, but his brother was on a service call and his mobile wasn't responding. "Bloodclaat!" he cursed, then remembered where he was.

Ganét Publishing was a rapidly expanding magazine publishing house based in Old Street near the City and he'd supplied a few machines to them in the past, mainly as cheap secondary equipment. With over 120 Apple Mac machines and a whole heap of other associated hardware, it would have been a nice gig to have but, unfortunately, a larger computer firm had got that one sown up. All Mac In-Touch was left with was the occasional crumb when someone needed a cheap machine installed quickly.

Now he was trying with limited success to get a middle range Mac working on the existing network. It was located in the office of Mrs Bramble and from the conversation he'd had with her on the phone, she'd sounded like her name: thorny. He'd not met the woman and didn't want to. That's what was worrying him. The arrangement had been that he'd have the machine installed and running before she got back at 11.30 from an appointment.

The office door was open but he was on his own and assumed it was okay to curse. He tried loading the software one more time before flinging his arms up in frustration.

"Bumbaclaat! Why don't you fucking work, eh?"

The exaggerated coughing cut his curse short. He looked up to see a young black woman standing in the open doorway with a pile of papers in her hand. He liked what he saw. She was immaculately dressed in a beige, double breasted trouser suit and white blouse. Her complexion was like molasses, and her face slim. High cheekbones and almond eyes, gave her the appearance of a sculpture carved from a piece of ebony. A soft bob encircled her face and she carried her slim frame with an air of class. In short, she was gorgeous. He didn't care how old she was or how tall she was. She seemed to require a category all of her own.

Michael was moved. Ganét chose it's secretaries well, he thought. He stood up quickly and apologised.

"Excuse me," he mumbled, "I'm not normally given to profanity, but I just can't get this rahtid… I mean, this software, to work. When your boss gets back she won't be too pleased."

The woman smiled politely and walked over to the filing cabinet, ignoring him while she filed her papers away. It was going to take more than the cold shoulder to dissuade Michael. He had already decided to strike up a conversation by any means necessary.

"If you don't mind me saying," he began confidently, "you look a little stressed. But you know I can relate to that. I spoke to your boss on the phone the other day and I can see why you're stressed. Bwoy, me can see why she called Bramble. The woman jus' cut me dead so!"

Michael's exaggerated Jamaican voice had its desired effect. The woman turned around and laughed. Sisters were usually impressed by the fluency with which he juxtaposed the Queen's English and patois. The inherent humour never failed to melt the coldest heart. Michael was pleased that the old charm wasn't letting him down.

"She's not like that at all," the woman said, coming to her boss' defence. "The way she sees it, she's here to do a job and social chit chat can wait for out of office hours. It's hard enough being a powerful woman in a man's world; you've got to make sure men take you seriously."

Michael nodded his head in agreement. Here was a woman who was articulate and confident. That always turned him on.

Michael tried his brother's mobile again and this time he got through. In a short time, the problem with the computer was resolved. He could now relax a little.

"Any chance of a coffee?" he called out to the secretary.

"White, one sugar."

She looked across at him and smiled.

"Oh sure, no problem. You go out of this room, turn left and by the reception there's a coffee machine. Could you get me a black coffee, no sugar. Thanks."

Michael felt sheepish. He walked to the door without his usual confident swagger.

"You said left to the reception?"

"That's correct. Ask someone if you get lost. Do you need some change?"

He felt like a schoolboy being sent out of the class. Michael returned with the coffees and saw her examining the newly installed computer.

During his walk to the coffee machine he'd sussed out the game plan and was determined he'd come out of this one on top. It was time to make his next move.

"Nice looking machine isn't it? You used a Mac before?" He didn't wait for her reply before moving to the back of the machine to switch it on. "This is the on/off switch and there's one on the front of the monitor."

"That's amazing! And all those pretty colours on the screen as well."

It sounded like sarcasm, but he wasn't sure. Maybe it was time to hit the ball a bit harder.

"Yeah, they're first rate machines these. It's got the Motorola 040 chip running at 33 megahertz and 8 ram and 160 megs on board."

She nodded her head, looking impressed. "Right. Of course."

Michael sensed it was nearly 'game, set and match'. He moved to make his next serve but was interrupted.

"In this spec sheet from Apple Mac, it says the LC 475 runs at 25 mega hertz and we did specify a 250 megabite hard disk when we ordered the machine from your company." She handed him a printed leaflet with details about the machine.

He felt victory ebb into the distance. He looked hard at the sheet before taking control of the computer's mouse to check the configuration of the hard disk. The machine had been fitted with a 250 megabite hard disk. It was an easy mistake to make but he knew he had to be gracious in defeat.

"My apologies, you're quite right. We have to deal with so many types of machine that even I sometimes get confused about what spec one machine or another has."

The woman flashed a triumphant smile. Michael grimaced.

"Hey, don't worry about it," she said, "we all make mistakes, don't we?"

He was trying to place the accent but couldn't quite suss it out. It was a refined London tone, but it seemed to have a little bit of the US or the Caribbean in there somewhere.

"I hope you don't mind me asking, but where are you from?"

"That's a very personal question," she teased. "But as you so kindly showed me how to switch on this computer, I'll tell you: South Wimbledon."

Michael smiled. He was happy to play along, after all he had brought it on himself.

"Right, funny. You know what I mean."

"My mother is from the Bahamas and my father is from Jamaica." Then she added in a Yankie accent: "And my ancestry is Fanti".

"Really, I'm supposed to go to Ghana, this year."

"You should, it's a gorgeous country, and its people are so astute."

"Yes, I've noticed."

She laughed and held a smile, as if to say "touché". *At least I've got her talking*. Michael sensed that now was the time to make his move.

"Listen I've got a friend of mine playing at Ronnie Scott's on Sunday night, would you like to come along?"

"Give me one good reason why I should accept your invitation?"

Michael hadn't prepared an answer for this one so he just opened his mouth and waited to hear what would come out.

"Because I truly believe we could have an enjoyable evening together, sharing some laughs and arguing over issues. Some genuine conversation for a change," he said, surprised by his own response.

"Good answer, nine out of ten for delivery," the woman announced with a smile. "I accept your invitation, but know this: I need a man that can show commitment. A man who is not afraid to show his true emotional side. A man who likes nature and riding naked in the forest." Michael's mouth dropped. The woman laughed. "Sunday night is fine, but you'd better be interesting company or I'll demand a refund."

Michael shook his head in exaggerated disbelief. He had never met a woman like this before.

"I might regret asking for this, but what's your number? Oh by the way my name's Michael Hughes."

She took out a business card from the desk and pressed it into his palm.

"I don't give out my home number to strangers. You can get me on my mobile. The number's on my card."

Michael swiftly turned on his heels and left the office, picking up his bag on the way. It wasn't until he reached the lift that he opened his hand to read the card.

"Oh man, oh man," he sighed, "this just ain't my day."

The card read 'Monica Bramble, Advertising Sales Director.'

The booming sounds of Shabba's 'Mr Loverman' were putting him off the task at hand.

"Please deejay. A man can't think with that noise going on."

Cynthia apologised and lowered the volume on the ghetto blaster. Sipping from an 'I Love Daddy' inscribed coffee mug, Josey strolled from Mac In-Touch's back office to take a break from mending a computer. His attention shifted to his brother who was at his desk studying a Russian translation dictionary and occasionally tapping the keys on the keyboard in front of him.

"Mikey, Mum says to say 'hi', and to tell you to eat properly. What skank are you up to now?"

"Ah, shit, when did she call? Remind me to call her tonight. This is no skank, just some shrewd business strategy."

Michael explained that he was creating a fake letterhead purporting to be that of the visiting Russian delegation. He would type out a letter saying the trip had been cancelled for a few weeks but they would fax details the next week about a new date of arrival.

All he needed to do was fax it to the Micro Chippie office, and Winston's your uncle! There would be no Micro Chippie rep to meet the Russians at Heathrow on Friday morning, but instead a very helpful salesman from the Mac In-Touch. A Mr Michael Hughes to be precise.

The plan seemed fool proof and the only way they could compete with the dodgy gear that Micro Chippie dealt in. Josey was not convinced.

"Cho' man! Is only you could come up wid a scheme like dis Michael. It'll end wid eye water." He didn't sound angry, more resolved to the fact that Michael was going to do it anyhow.

Although born in London, like his brother, Josey frequently switched between his slight cockney accent and a Jamaican one, as the mood took him. He offered his brother some technical advice.

"You know on their fax paper it will print our company name and fax number unless you re-programme our machine?"

"Don't worry big brother everyt'ing is copasetic. I've got that one well-sorted, trust me. I know this girl Natashka, who I had a lickle t'ing wid. She works at the Russian Trade Delegation office. I'm getting her to fax it. It couldn't look more authentic, wouldn't you agree? Now, tell me boss, am I a genius or what?"

Josey had to laugh at the sheer bare-faced cheek of Michael's plan. He touched fists with his younger brother.

"Alright junior, respeck." But he added, "If t'ings go wrong jus' remember who ah warn you."

"Don't worry boss, we ah go nice up the dance, sweet", replied Michael.

Josey finished his coffee and started back to the task at hand. He stopped for a moment and turned round with a grin on his face.

"Natashka? Tell me Mikey is there any woman in London who you've not boned?"

Michael laughed. Josey's eyes met Cynthia's briefly. She raised one eyebrow then turned back to her computer screen with a smirk on her face.

The satisfied grin on the face of the middle-aged businessman in the black Mercedes got him vexed. They stared each other out for a moment, but the traffic on the other side of the Bayswater Road started moving again and the Merc disappeared. He felt like cursing the man, but that wouldn't have done any good at this precise moment. Michael climbed back in his BM and shoved the speeding ticket into the glove compartment with all the others. In his rearview mirror he saw the police Rover pull out and head off in the direction of Notting Hill Gate. To add insult to injury, one of the two women officers gave him a smile and a wave as they drove past. He threw her a miserable, screwed-up look in return.

Boy, he was pissed off. He was sure he wasn't doing more than forty up Park Lane and he was even polite to them. But they still gave him a ticket. And it was the white one who would have let him off but that stone-faced black Sergeant made sure she gave him a ticket. Her man must have pissed her off so bad this morning, that she was taking out her vengeance on the whole of black manhood. Cho'! He was well vexed.

He started up the car, still reflecting on the incident.

Cho' man! A black woman too. What's the world coming to, man? Is woman run t'ings now. Rahtid!

He was still cursing when he pulled up at Mac In-Touch some time later, having just dropped off the fax at the Russian Trade office. Inside the shop, two well-built white men in bomber jackets and jeans were waiting. He sensed trouble.

"Michael, these gentlemen are here to see you."

"Are you Michael Hughes?" asked the thirtysomething one with the crew cut.

Thanks to Cynthia, he could hardly deny who he was. He had no choice but to switch to automatic salesman mode.

"That's correct. How can I be of assistance to you?" He offered his hand and the man, obviously embarrassed, shook it half-heartedly.

"Well, Sir, we work for TGB Finance and we're here to collect your BMW 318i. It appears you are behind on your payments and despite two warning letters to this effect, you have made no attempt to contact the office. I'm very sorry about this. Could I have the keys please? Is it the one outside getting a parking ticket?"

Michael looked out at the black woman traffic warden walking off. He had to think fast.

"There must be some mistake. Look, my secretary is new here; she probably forgot to send off the payment." He came closer to the car collector and spoke in a loud whisper. "You know these youngsters. Their minds aren't on the job. I blame it on crack."

In the background, he heard Cynthia kiss her teeth.

"Look, if I write you out a cheque now, I'm sure we can settle this unfortunate mix up."

The man looked at his colleague who nodded and said, "Plastic".

"It'll have to be a credit card, Sir."

Michael produced his Barclaycard and signed.

"I don't like being used as an excuse for your money mix-ups, Michael." Cynthia was seething. "Also, I do not, I repeat, I DO NOT have anything to do with crack, because if I did, I certainly wouldn't be able to run this office on my own with no help."

Michael apologised and conceded that the crack comment was out of order, but she was far from forgiving him.

"Okay, I'm off. Remember I told you about the Parents' evening at Marcus' school," Josey announced suddenly.

Michael said goodbye to his brother who disappeared out of the shop door with a bundle of papers. He was back in a moment.

"Mikey, don't forget to send Diana a birthday card. Anyway I'll see you both later."

The tension between Michael and Cynthia didn't ease any once Josey had gone. If anything it got worse. She chose to ignore him totally. Michael watched her for a moment as she typed a letter, before deciding to walk over and massage her shoulders from behind. Cynthia shrugged him off firmly.

"Move yourself, Michael. Don't bother trying to sweet me up."

He persevered with the massage. This time her resistance was weaker. Eventually, he could feel her anger subsiding under his fingers.

"Come on baby, don't be like that," he said soothingly, "I said I was sorry."

"Yeah, well it ain't very nice for your boss to say you're a crack addict. And it don't look too clever on you either for employing me."

Michael knew the charm was working.

"Sorry, is all that I can say."

He sang the lyrics from an old reggae tune to further soften her up. He bent down and kissed her on the neck which brought a giggle.

"Michael! Behave yourself. Anyone could just walk in." He smiled, but simply kissed her again, on her shoulder this time. "Oh Michael. You're bad yuh know. You should be more like your brother. A respectable man." He kissed her again. This time, much lower. "Michael. I don't know what you think you're gonna find down there. Michael. At least you could shut up the shop first."

He knew it was unprofessional to mix business with pleasure but Michael was like an addict, he had to have his fix. Cynthia had only been working at the shop a week before he first got off with her at his yard. She'd fancied him from the moment she first saw him and knew she was as much to blame for their sex romps. But they chose not to tell Josey about their horizontal relationship, because they knew he would go mad. Maybe she should have stopped Michael there and then, but as Shabba says, the man really was 'wicked inna bed'. He was a dog, but as she told a friend, 'that bow-wow can really hit the G spot'.

With the shutters of the shop secured, Michael returned to the task at hand.

"Michael, this is crazy, I've got to meet a friend up West in an hour…"

Cynthia was already removing her panties and hitching up her skirt. She sat on the edge of her desk, her legs wide apart with each foot on a chair. Using her right hand, she slowly pulled open the lips of her vagina to tease her man.

"All right. Come on Michael, you know what I like."

She opened and closed her legs. One moment teasing him with her pink flesh, the next withdrawing her offer. Every few movements she would remove her right forefinger and lick it in a slow deliberate fashion with the tip of her tongue. Then she would return it to her pussy, stroking her clitoris so he could see it harden with her gentle touch.

For a woman so young, she knew exactly how to turn a man on, thought Michael. His prick was so stiff in his pants he was in agony. He decided to play it cool. He didn't want this 'young gal' thinking that she called the shots. He was after all her boss.

He slowly and deliberately removed his suit, taking great care to make sure each item was properly folded and neatly deposited on the desk behind him.

"Michael. I'm gonna be late. Hurry up!"

He laughed, but it was not long before his large strong hands were gripping her inner thighs and his tongue working its magic in her pussy. Cynthia moaned in ecstasy, her head resting on the top shelf of a metal letter tray. Cold, tingly shivers ran over her body as the tip of his tongue darted backwards and forwards over her clitoris, teasing it into a throbbing erect state amidst the mixture of saliva and pussy juices mingled with her black pubic hairs.

Now Michael was standing. He removed a condom from his wallet and unfolded the lubricated rubber sheath over the firm length of his cock. Cynthia waited in anticipation for the moment, her wide eyes alert as his left thumb opened her vagina and his right hand guided his wood into her wetness. A mixed feeling of pain and pleasure gripped her and she let out a cry that signified both. Her sex was stretched by the girth of his large cock and as he pushed it gently, but deep inside her, she was reminded of how painful it could be. The ridge of his head was now making its way deep inside her as her vaginal juices lubricated his tool, the feeling of tightness subsided as waves of pleasure washed over her.

Michael's mind focussed onto her panting as he matched her rhythm with the movement of his hips. He became more and more aroused as Cynthia's high-pitched shrieks urged him to "Fuck me harder!" and his pelvis responded with sudden violent thrusts.

Theirs was not an act of tender love-making. This was raw, dirty, randy, physical fucking at its best. Unrestricted and uncontrollable. He scooped her up and lay her down on the desk, still working her into a frenzy.

Soon a huge orgasmic tidal wave washed through her and she let out a loud squeal as she climaxed. Michael pumped more violently and felt his legs quiver and his head evaporate. His pelvis went into automatic spasm as he shot his load.

FIVE

He had slipped into a dream-like trance where he saw himself in the aisle of a supermarket, pushing a food laden shopping trolley with a toddler in the red plastic seat. Next to him was a fat woman nagging and telling him he was 'wotless'. When he turned and looked, the woman was Jackie saying the same thing over and over again.

"Michael did you hear what I said…? Michael did you hear what I said…?"

Suddenly, he returned back to reality and looked across to his companion.

"You're in another world tonight, Michael. Did you hear what I said?"

"Barbara, I'm sorry. My head is so mashed up these days with thinking about work. Apologies, what was it you were saying?"

"I just wanted to know if you were ready to order, that's all."

Michael glanced quickly at the menu and ordered Peking duck and special fried rice.

After his earlier vigorous bout of activity with Cynthia in the office, he felt in no mood for a dinner date. But Barbara would have been pissed off if he'd cancelled. She was one of those sensitive women who easily felt unloved. If he blew her out she'd act as if the world had come to an end. He liked Barbara, but he should have manners her from day one instead of getting himself into the difficult situation he found himself in with her now.

From that first weekend when Barbara had insisted that they drive to Ikea to choose furniture for her flat together, he should have seen it coming. Barbara was a woman who wanted a husband to do all those husband things with, like going to Ikea on a Saturday. He should have told her there and then which way the land lay. But he didn't. She was a nice woman and he didn't want to hurt her feelings. He should have told her, 'look baby all I want from you is the occasional night out and some sexual healing'. He should have told her about the other women. But he hadn't and now, six months down the line, she thought she was the 'someone special' in his life. As far as she was concerned, he was her man. She wanted that special relationship so much, she ignored the signs indicating what kind of man Michael was or in any case refused to accept what was obvious.

She had just turned thirty and was still single. She had started working at eighteen after her A-levels, and had thrown herself into her work with all her energy. Her efforts quickly paid off and she rose from secretary, to earning a good salary as manager of a large, prestigious city recruitment agency. Now all that was missing was that special man and children. Two of her younger sisters were already settled with kids and she was afraid that life was leaving her behind.

The Chinese waiter rapidly cut the duck up and lay the other dishes on the giant Ming-style plate in the middle of the table.

The *Ho Hing* in Crouch End was one of the best Chinese restaurants in north London and was a convenient ten minutes away from Barbara's two-bedroomed Edwardian flat. Michael was not really in the mood for dinner or Barbara's company. Her motherly ways were suffocating at the best of times, but especially now.

"Is everything all right, Michael? You seem very distant this evening. Is it anything I've done? You would say if there's anything I've done to annoy you, wouldn't you? Is the food alright? Shall I put some more rice on your plate?"

"Barbara. Everything is fine. I told you, I've a lot on my mind." His tone was harsher than he'd intended and she lowered her eyes, with a sullen expression. He could see she was upset.

"I'm sorry, Michael. I didn't mean to pressure you."

"It's okay. You don't need to apologise. Everything is fine."

For the next few minutes they ate in silence, but Michael sensed that there was something she was dying to say and wondered when it would come. She eventually rested her chop sticks on the table and raised her head.

"Michael, I have a proposition to make. I know things are a bit tight for you at the moment financially, with the mortgage and so forth. So I was thinking, why don't you rent out your house for six months or so and come and live at my place? You can have your own room and come and go as you want; you don't have to pay rent, and I'll do all the cooking. What do you think Michael?"

Michael clicked his fingers.

"Waiter, can I have the bill please?"

SIX

Ivan Andropov was in good spirits this morning. Like his three other colleagues, this was to be his first visit to London and they were determined that they would do good business and enjoy themselves. They were the new style of Russian businessmen. All aged in their early and mid-thirties, they dressed in sharp Italian suits and embraced all things hi-tech and Western. They carried their mobile phones proudly and two of the party had brought their Toshiba laptop computers along to complete the image.

Even though it was still only 9.00am they had nearly consumed the entire contents of a litre bottle of Vodka. The Aeroflot jet was conspicuous by its lack of fellow passengers, and this served as an encouragement for the party to sing their old army songs, learned when they were army conscripts during the Soviet occupation of Afghanistan.

It was in the final weeks of the military withdrawal from Afghanistan that the comrades started their business activities, trading soviet military equipment for hashish with the local Mujahidin. The hash was transported to a contact in East Germany who then moved it into the West, which set the Russians up with a large cash flow of roubles. They were now respected 'commodity brokers', buying and selling Western goods as well as Russian raw materials. With expensive apartments near Red Square, they were among the first private citizens in Moscow to own BMWs and Mercedes.

In Blackheath, Michael was in a sombre mood. This was all a bit too much like déjà vu for his liking. At least this time he knew what was on the other side of the fence. Once again, he was having to sneak out of the back door of his own house, early in the morning, like a thief. But he was certainly not opening the front door to two dodgy white guys. They looked like the same ones who had called the other morning, but he wasn't going to open the door to ask them if they were.

This time, however, he was better equipped to tackle this early morning assault course. He placed the rug from the study on the top of his neighbour's fence and carefully pulled himself up on to the top. He performed a perfect landing on the lawn, avoiding the muddy flowerbed. Again, the rug over the next fence made sure that there weren't going to be any ripped Armani suits this morning. As he rolled up the rug and tucked it under his arm, he was still to face the neighbour's shocked expression at the French windows. She looked even more incredulous this time, as he walked down the path at the side of the house. Michael gave his familiar smile and thumbs up greeting before hot-footing it to the BMW.

The traffic on the way to Heathrow was fairly free-flowing for a Friday morning and it allowed his mind to wonder as he pondered his female predicament. There was nothing he could do about the situation with Jackie. Only fate could deal with that right now; that one was best kept at the bottom of the 'worry' tray. Although he'd only just met her, Nadia somehow felt that he and she were an 'item'. How could he have allowed that to happen? At least she was in Jamaica for another few weeks, so that could go in the 'pending' tray. Barbara was a problem, most definitely. That needed to be at the top of the 'worry' tray because he needed to have it sorted and fast. Okay he'd made a mistake there, but he wasn't going to lose any sleep if she got upset when he broke the bad news to her. *Maybe I should jus' dump it in the 'why worry' tray?*

There was just one other blot on the landscape, under the name of Shantelle.

She had called late last night just after he got in, but Michael was in no mood to talk to her. He left her talking away on the answerphone, declaring how much she loved and missed him. He'd not seen her for a couple of weeks and had already told her he was too busy with work to see her for a while. He hadn't told her he was seeing other women, but then, he'd never denied it. It wasn't his fault if she didn't ask, that was her business, and it was his business what he did. Shantelle however, was a women who was 'on the edge' and Michael realised that there could be some serious ructions if she found out. Cho', what was he worried for? The problem was hers. *If she don't like it then she can jus' gwan.*

His mental deliberations were cut short by the large silver Mercedes that cruised past in the outside lane of the motorway. The diplomatic number plate and the black, green and yellow, colours of the small flag on the bonnet indicated that this was an embassy car of an African state. Michael wasn't too concerned about that because his attention was focused on the beautiful black woman in the back reading a copy of Vogue. He increased his speed to keep level with the Merc and honked his horn to attract her attention. Michael gave her his sexiest smile. With a look of disdain on her face, she resumed reading her magazine and for good measure drew the curtain on the side window.

He'd not noticed how quickly he'd been driving and how fast he was catching up with the car in front of him in his lane. He got close enough to make out the name of the supplying garage before he slammed on the brakes and swerved into the outside lane. Within seconds he heard the familiar blaring of a police siren. As he waited on the motorway's hard shoulder, he noticed in his rear view mirror, the familiar figure of 'that' same black woman sergeant exit from the driver's side of the white patrol car.

The Terminal 3 car park seemed rather familiar and his eyes searched around for any green Range Rovers. Despite the pull by the police, he had arrived at Heathrow with time to spare. He thanked Jah that the policewoman had been in a benevolent mood that morning and had only given him a verbal warning. He couldn't afford any more points on his license right now.

He took his small cardboard sign which had 'IVAN

ANDROPOV' written on it in black felt pen and made his way to the Arrivals lounge. He figured that all he would need to do now was wait for his Russian visitors and, with his salesman skills, Mac In-Touch would be back rolling where they were in the boom times. He positioned himself by the chrome hand-rail at the exit barriers and was about to hold up his sign when his stomach dropped. On the other side of the barrier was a flash, suited sales-looking guy, holding a sign saying 'IVAN ANDROPOV'. His mind searched for answers. It found one. Natashka. The silly bitch hadn't sent the fax. Shit! All week he'd tried to phone her to make sure she'd sent it, but she was always out on appointments. How could she have neglected it? He was angry and cursed the woman under his breath. *And to think of the good sex I gave that bitch.*

Michael clenched his fists tightly. He'd have to think fast. Too much was riding on this horse for it to stumble at this point in the race. But what could he do? What the hell could he do? Suddenly he smiled. *Yes Jah! Jah live. Yes, yes.*

He took his mobile phone out and called directory enquires. He scribbled the number down and just as quickly was dialling again.

"Hello is that the information desk? Could you page the representative from Micro Chippie meeting a delegation from Russia. Could you tell him to go to the information desk and wait there. The Russians will meet him there. That's right, ask him to wait there. It's all been arranged. It's rather urgent so I'd appreciate it if you could do it ASAP. Okay, thanks a lot. Cheers."

Michael didn't have to wait long. In less than a minute, the announcement came over the airport announcement speakers and he could see the Flash Harry walk down the stairs to the Information Desk.

"Everyt'ing sweet inna the dance," Michael told himself with a smile.

Half an hour later a group of red-faced, burly Russians were squeezed into Michael's BMW, cruising down the M4 into central London. They had been surprised to see a black man waiting for them, but they seemed delighted at the novelty value of meeting a genuine Afro-Saxon if nothing else.

"Da. Bob Marley. Good. Big fan," Ivan had told him as they drove out of the car park. Michael slipped a raw, dancehall soundclash tape in the cassette deck and from the cheers of appreciation from the Muscovites, he was sure he'd be wrapping this deal up quicker than he had expected. He had also taken the trouble of bringing some top grade sensi with him and the delegation were soon building up on their motorway journey. While they were savouring the spliffs, Michael then handed the Mac In-Touch catalogues so they could get familiar with the machinery and accessories on offer.

"In Afghanistan we smoke good hashish. This hashish good too," said an appreciative Ivan.

At the Mac In-Touch's offices, the Russians were even more surprised to find that the company was a black-owned business. Josey made his introductions and got down to telling them what the company could offer them equipment-wise. One of the Russians had wandered away from the discussion and was clearly more interested in the company's other 'assets'. The Russian had taken a shine to Cynthia and had found a seat for himself on her desk, where he was teaching her Russian and she was teaching him Brixtonian.

"Wee-ked. Da?"

Cynthia giggled.

"No, da. 'Wicked'. Yeah? W-i-c-k-e-d."

After Josey had filled the delegation in on the technical details, Michael took over and gave the sales talk about Mac In-Touch's expertise and contacts and why an East-West connection would be of great mutual benefit. Michael's direct no-nonsense style of delivery was well-suited to the Russians who clearly did not suffer from the sensibilities of the English. They were a plain-speaking bunch, not interested in any bullshit. They interpreted life in cold roubles and wasted no time in getting straight to the nitty gritty.

In a surprisingly short time, a deal was worked out where they would pay for a large hardware order in cash. US dollars to be precise. They would return in three weeks time to pick up the order in person, and they would then settle up in cash. For Michael, it was the sort of yard-style business deal that was a refreshing change to all the 30 days credit stuff that they normally had to deal with. He produced a bottle of Cockspur rum and they toasted the new business relationship. Everything had been signed sealed and delivered so quickly that Michael could now relax for the day and play tourist guide to the Russians who were anxious to get going to paint the town red. Michael had to practically drag the other Russian away from Cynthia's desk, who by now was getting a bit too friendly with her.

"Ain't he cute? He looks just like Arnold Schwarzenegger in Red Heat", Cynthia said of the 6' 4" Eastern visitor as he left the office.

They set off to see the tourist attractions of central London, paying visits to the Houses of Parliament, Buckingham Palace, St. Paul's Cathedral, and Trafalgar Square. The Russians were particularly keen to sample the capitalistic delights of the city so Michael took them shopping at some of the department stores on Oxford Street before heading to the world famous Harrods in Knightsbridge. The Russians weren't doing any thing by halves either. They stopped of at a bank and changed over $70,000 into sterling, between them. At Harrods, they acted like kids at the proverbial candy store. Every few minutes they would seize some designer product or another and head for the cash till. Dizzy from the thought of so much money being spent in so few minutes, Michael noticed a store detective following them around. He sucked his teeth and proceeded to escort the Russians to the shoe section.

Their spending spree over, Michael took the party to the Dorchester Hotel where they had booked rooms for the night. It was 6.00pm and it seemed an appropriate time for him to bid farewell. But the Russians would have none of it.

"Ve vont to go where Africans go. Ve vont to go Brex-Tone."

Michael laughed. "You want to go to Brixton?" He had a surprised look on his face. The Russians smiled and nodded in unison.

"Da."

Despite the January weather, Brixton Road was a teeming hive of activity at that time of the evening. Locals, commuters heading to pastures more southerly, concert goers, and clubbers were out in force, giving the place a lively and cosmopolitan feel. The Russians were clearly enjoying the vibe.

"Voo is Jay Shake?" enquired Ivan.

Michael followed the path of the Russian's gaze to a fly poster near the tube station.

"Oh, 'Jah Shaka'. He's a… um… um musician. He runs a sound system." He knew his explanation wouldn't be that clear, but the Russians nodded their heads anyway as though they understood.

Their mini-guided tour of Brixton continued, with Michael pointing out local places of interest. He told them about the history of black settlement in the area, the heavy policing that lead to the riots, the best food shops, how to cook plantain and how the area was changing. The visitors had taken a real liking to ragga music thanks to Michael, and said they wanted to take some tapes back to Russia. Michael pulled up outside a Reggae shop and stepped in with the Russians, to help them select a wide assortment of sounds. The puzzled look on the dread's face behind the counter when they entered, soon changed to a smile when they bought over £300's worth of tapes and CD's.

The next stop was the Caribbean takeaway on Acre Lane. Double parking outside the busy food shop, Michael treated the Russians to some tasty home-style curried goat and rice and peas. The Russians soon got the hang of the plastic forks and foil containers, as they devoured their food. Washed down with some bottles of Dragon Stout, they enjoyed the culinary fare tremendously and asked for the recipe.

Late in the evening they ended up at the Brixtonian, where the Russians insisted on tasting every different rum in the house. As the bar claimed to serve the largest selection of 'rhums' in Britain, Michael had a long wait. The party lounged on wicker chairs, generally chilling out after what had been a full and tiring day. Michael proposed a toast to commemorate this newly cemented development in East-West relations.

"The Cold War is over. It's time to chill," he announced with his glass raised. The humour was lost somewhere in the language gap, but all the same the Russians slammed their glasses together and gave a hearty "Respek" before downing the potent liquor in one.

For a moment Michael was in reflective mood. He had enjoyed playing tour guide to the Easterners and he had particularly liked showing them around Brixton. They in turn had relished their foray into deepest south London. Michael turned to Ivan.

"You know, there are many English people in London who will never come to Brixton. These people are happy to live in their own little worlds and think they know what's happening. You've come all they way from Russia, yet you're here in Brixton enjoying yourselves. It's a funny old world, I'm telling you."

Michael rarely got this philosophical about life, but this day had got him thinking. While Ivan's English wasn't good enough for him to understand humour, he understood the full meaning of Michael's observation. He translated for his comrades and they sombrely nodded their heads in agreement.

"Old Russian proverb: 'if you cannot travel with open mind, do not begin the journey'. Ivan seemed serious for the first time that evening.

Michael understood where the Russian was coming from and nodded his head.

"Yeah, respect man. Respect."

SEVEN

"And I'm telling you man, the white one would have let me off. It was the black woman who wanted to nail my ass. Fe true rasta."

Alex Henderson listened sympathetically as Michael recalled his speeding ticket ordeal during the week. He rested the weights on the support and sat up before giving his moral support.

"I tell you man, you gotta watch out for some of the sisters these days. I tell you they'll fuck you up."

Michael voiced his agreement with that sentiment.

Social engagements permitting, Saturday morning was a regular session at Hackney's Lee Valley Sports Centre for Michael and his spar Alex. Both men had an interest in working out in the gym and the weekly session afforded a good opportunity to keep updated with their respective news.

They had known each other for the best part of ten years having become friends through Sunday morning football. They would pretend to play football for a couple of hours, when in fact the game was merely a prelude to the lengthy discussions the team would have in the local pub. The Simba Lions had long since broken up, but many of the old team had kept in contact. Alex, the perennial bachelor, had his own mobile phone business in Bethnal Green. He was a year older than Michael and, like his spar, he had little desire to 'settle down'. He enjoyed playing the field and found Michael an agreeable teamster with whom he could discuss form and game strategy.

"Yeah Mikey. Check dat t'ing over there. Nice t'ing ain't it?"

In conspiratorial whispers the two men eyed a woman tackling a gruelling uphill section on the step machine.

"Seen. I wouldn't mind getting to know her." Michael kept his eyes on the undulations of her buttocks."

"I'm one step ahead of you, star. Her name's Simone. She works up Hackney Town Hall, but I think some brother over

55

there is checking her."

They shrugged their shoulders with a sigh, before continuing their discussion about the plight of the black bachelor, then finally getting back to the business at hand. Training with a friend not only made the exercise more enjoyable, but each one spurred the other on to push their bodies further and harder. Once in the gym, the two men were intensely competitive, each trying to lift greater loads than the next man. Although a good six inches shorter than his sidekick and not as heavy, Alex could match him pound for pound and intended to make sure it stayed that way.

For two hours, the two grunted and strained, pushing themselves to do one more rep. Once they were feeling totally flexed they called it a day and headed for the changing rooms to enjoy the simple pleasure of a relieving hot shower. Later, they sat in the centre's café sipping on orange juice. The compadres discussed the runnings for the evening; Alex had planned a surprise.

"You know Andrea who lives up by me? Well she's arranged for her friend Sharon to come round. She's getting some drinks in, some herb and food. She says she'll see what develops but she reckons her mate is game."

Michael's eyes lit up. He could always trust Alex to get some action going.

It was through Alex that Michael and Andrea had met and they had enjoyed a number of sexual encounters across the months. How they first got to know each other would always bring a smile to Michael's face. Having only just met her at a party a week before, Alex turned up at Andrea's flat one night with Michael. It was only meant to be a flying visit, but soon they were all drinking brandy and smoking spliffs. One thing led to another and before long they were both in Andrea's bed, laced around her naked body. Andrea confessed that she'd always had a fantasy about a 'menage à trois' and she was exhilarated that it had finally happened.

It didn't end with Andrea either. Alex and Michael teamed up on two subsequent occasions to complete the triangle for two other women.

"Alex, have I been meeting the wrong women or have black women changed?"

His spar looked puzzled. "What d'you mean?"

"Well star, one minute the women want you to take control, then the next they're pissed off because you haven't let them dictate the runnings. Two-twos now, her body's crying out for the 'out-of-the-ordinary' shit, but she still looks shocked when you suggest it. A brother just don't know where he stands."

Alex agreed. "It's true. A lot of women won't accept that these things did ah gwan back in the days. I've known some pretty kinky black women in my time, but they tended not to be too up front about it, that's all."

"Example?"

"Example: you remember that church gal, Debbie?"

Michael held a blank expression.

"You know the one who was friendly with Danny's sister Cho' man, don't go crazy on me, you know that Debbie that worked at Barclays." Michael finally nodded in recognition. Alex was relieved. "Well anyway, for a lickle time I was checking her. I can tell you she was one freaky-deaky chickadee. She liked to be spanked, do the anal bit, the works. But she was only like that when she found out I was just as kinky as her. Bwoy, I had some serious fucked-up times with that gal. I was forever going back for more."

"Detail, my friend, detail. You can't leave me hanging like this."

Breaking into a homeboy Yankie accent to entertain his captive audience, Alex concluded.

"I'm talking shit I'd be embarrassed to tell you about. And I know you're one fucked up, kinky motherfucker."

The two fell about in raucous laughter. Then Alex started to speak in more hushed tones when he realised that their laughter was attracting the attention of the other café users.

"Tonight should be a good one. I don't know what her friend looks like or if she's down with the programme, let's just watch the ride. But anyway Mikey, some of the women I've seen you with, I know you really care what the bitch looks like." Alex oozed sarcasm

"You're funny, man. Don't let me haffe remind you 'bout the Beast Woman from Dalston."

Alex's face dropped; embarrassment caused him to shuffle in his seat and stare at Michael hard.

"Cho' man. I was charged at the time and the dance was dark."

The standard response to such indiscretions allowed Alex to squirm out of a further rendition of a story he would rather forget. The guys were just jesting, the atmosphere was light and the jokes flowed.

The cool sounds of George Benson wafted around the house. Michael sprawled on the sofa chuckling to himself, watching an old episode of 'The Cosby Show' when the kids were still cute and the observations were still sharp. In a white T shirt and grey cotton jogging bottoms, he was unwinding after the morning's gym exertions. It seemed so rare for him to get a moment of relaxation these days. He was making the most of it. His eyes caught the business card on the carved wooden coffee table and he was reminded about his plans for Sunday night.

'Monica Bramble, Advertising Sales Director'. He looked at the card's design for a moment and recalled his rather embarrassing encounter with her during the week.

He picked up the phone and dialled the digits in one rhythmic sequence.

"Ah, hi... Is Monica there please." The male voice surprised him. He wondered if he'd dialled the wrong number, but asked for her anyway. "Just say that it's Michael from the computer company."

A woman's voice came on the line.

"Hello."

"Hi Monica, it's me, Michael, the guy who installed your computer. Am I interrupting anything...? So who's the geezer that answered the phone...? Okay, I'm sorry, the question was just out of curiosity... Yes, I do know what happened to the cat. End of subject, okay... No, I wont be this nosey tomorrow. So can you still make Ronnie Scott's...? Nice one. Okay I tell you what, I'll meet you outside at 8.00pm sharp... Nah don't worry, I'll not only be on time, I'll be early... Yeah, but I don't deal wid no 'black man time' business. Rest assured of that... You may live to eat those words, and they won't taste too good with the humble pie, either... A'right. Lickle more."

Michael pushed the ariel down on the cordless phone and placed it back on the unit, still smiling from his verbal jousting with Monica. He lounged back in the sofa feeling pleased with himself.

It was a straightforward drive from Blackheath to Hackney. Two minutes to the Shooter's Hill roundabout then right on to the Blackwall tunnel approach road. From there it was plain sailing all the way to the 'People's Republic' — as Michael had styled the left-wing Labour borough. It made him wonder what his morning visitors were doing now. They had caught an in their Red Square apartments for have been now. Michael imagined them in some good few hours, knocking back vodka and telling the comrades Moscow bar about the Brixton nightlife. The image of Ivan in his large blue Mercedes, cruising past Gorky Park with the window down, Buju pumping from the car's sound system, was nothing short of comical. The look on the faces of his fellow Muscovites would be something to see. 'Respek Ivan, Respek.'

He found a parking space a few doors from the flat in Hackney's Glyn Road and noticed Alex's black Saab convertible opposite. Although he was always complaining about how hard business was, Alex always had to make sure he was driving an exceptional car. Glyn Road was one of those typical roads in Hackney where most of the three-storey Victorian houses had been converted into flats. Several of the windows had net curtains with trims and frills. Candelabra light fittings revealed front rooms filled with ornaments, glass cabinets and photographs of 'back home' and babies. This was very much a black area, though the occasional stripped pine, interior designed household was dotted among a row of long established black residences.

Andrea was born and bred in Hackney and was in no hurry to leave the borough. Her two-bedroomed maisonette was owned by a local housing association and was home to her and her six year old daughter.

Michael pressed the bell and a familiar face opened the door.

"Hello darling, how are you? Come in."

Andrea gave Michael a hug and led him downstairs to the lounge where Alex observed Sharon building one of her legendary 'jumbo' spliffs.

Andrea poured Michael a drink and asked what he'd been doing, lately. She had a laid-back personality which made people feel at ease. Down to earth and petite, she had a warm comforting aura about her. What Michael liked about Andrea most was her vibe. Her small mouth seemed to be in a permanent smile. He vibe made her approachable. Michael also liked her which made her cool, relaxed and matter-of-fact about to sex, she was enjoyed it and was not prepared to apolog*le thing. She saw no need for inhibitions or games either; she that. She she liked and was happy to demand it. That she was bi-sexual held no problems for her either. She believed that deep within our sub-conscious most people have the will to love both sexes. Andrea always liked to talk about all her bi-sexual relationships with black women and reckoned it was becoming more and more common. Michael never liked to hear that, it meant a whole other group to compete with.

Besides it was a 'waste' of womanhood.

Andrea had met Sharon through working for an insurance brokers in Liverpool Street. Although nothing had happened between them, she got the vibe that Sharon was willing to try anything at least once.

"Michael, you must feel that every woman on this planet wants to fall down at your feet."

"I'm not saying that, but 'oman must know when she got somet'ing good standing in front of her."

"I don't believe you, Michael. Honestly. Your dick ain't made of gold you know. There are other pleasures in life."

Michael and Andrea moved out of the kitchen and into the lounge. Sharon looked up to hear the tail end of their discussion as they entered. A tall, lightish-skinned girl in her mid-twenties, Sharon was a lively jokey person who saw life as a one chance affair. As a 'nineties girl' she didn't intend to wait for opportunity to knock. She would open the door and drag it in. From the way she was sitting on his lap cracking jokes and using very bold gestures, she and Alex were obviously happily charged.

They all sat around smoking spliffs, drinking and making happy. As the mood became more and more relaxed, Alex started to kiss Sharon on the cheek then on her mouth. Within a short time, his hand was sliding up her jumper and fondling her breasts.

Michael sat next to Andrea on the sofa, appreciating the show. He enjoyed watching people having sex. It was a huge turn-on. He put it down to a childhood experience when as an eight-year-old, he had spied on his uncle and a girlfriend having sex at a wedding party. He vividly remembered how his small penis became erect as he watched the middle-aged man pulsate on top of the young woman.

Alex had removed Sharon's jumper and bra and was now running his tongue over her right nipple. They were of an unusual largeness and stood erect. She was enjoying the pleasures of Alex's stimulation. Michael felt his cock rise at every move of his friend's tongue. Andrea was likewise transfixed by the spectacle, finding it far more entertaining than any naughty video. She stretched her leg across Michael's and began to nestle her toes in his crotch. She couldn't help but notice his stiffened member protruding from his trousers, as she slid her hand into her black leggings and started to play with herself.

On the other side of the room, Alex was now naked and removing Sharon's panties. She sat on the armchair with her legs apart, each one dangling over the side of the chair's arms. On his knees, Alex inserted two fingers into her pussy and slowly moved them backwards and forwards, as she kneaded her breasts. Her pelvis moved in rhythm with his fingers which he occasionally pulled out in order to stimulate her clitoris with a wet forefinger.

Michael and Andrea sat on the sofa blissfully glued to this spectacle of decadent sex. Michael had pulled out his penis from his jeans and was slowly working his wood to the brink of climax. Similarly, Andrea had freed herself from the burden of her leggings and underwear and she sat with only her black sweatshirt on, masturbating frenetically.

There was a definite symmetry to the occasion. On one side of the room sat the voyeurs and on the other, the exhibitionists. Each couple fed off the other, one action causing a reaction, in an equation that steadily raised the sexual charge in the room.

Sharon reached out to feel Alex's firm cock. Alex took his cue and raised his pelvis to enable her to manipulate his penis more easily. She played with it in the palm of her hand, allowing her fingers to roam around his balls and shaft. Her dexterity was as much for her own pleasure as for the observers nearby. She made every move slow, deliberate and clearly visible. With exaggerated slow movement, she pulled his foreskin back. With the tip of her tongue extended, she licked the head of his organ. Again in a slow and deliberate manner, she brought her feet down to the floor and pushed her hips down towards him. Alex wasn't sure what she was about to do so he just lay back and watched the ride. She brought his penis towards her, pulling back her lips to reveal her aroused clitoris.

"Do you want to be fucked?"

Before he could respond, Sharon had swallowed his penis in her throbbing sex. Alex gasped with delight as she proceeded to work his cock. He was overwhelmed. This was a new experience. When she pulled him out his soul seemed to sink. With her right hand, Sharon gripped the shaft of his penis and started to wank him with increasing vigour. The small, gold bracelet on her wrist caught the light from a nearby candle and glinted. Alex stood with his eyes closed, his hands resting on his hips. After an enjoyable while he stopped her, worried he was about to shoot his load.

Alex wasted no time. After preparing his manhood with a rubber sheath, he lifted Sharon with one arm and wrapped her legs around him. They turned, allowing him to sit in the chair. He carefully lowered her onto his penis. With his forearm rested along her spine, his right hand gripped her buttock. Slowly she worked herself up and down on his wood, lifting herself up then pushing it down hard on his penis. Alex gripped her left buttock tightly and inserted the middle finger deep into her ass. Within moments his body was jerking as he came violently. As Sharon raised herself up to her feet, Alex slumped back in the chair exhausted. She stood looking down at him like a warrior standing over her slain opponent.

Realising that her friend was in need of some stimulation now that Alex was temporarily out of action, Andrea peeled off her sweatshirt and went over to stand behind Sharon. Wrapping her arms around Sharon, she played with her nipples. Seeing them made Michael horny. The women's contrasting skin colours and body shapes made a pleasing spectacle. Andrea's large, bouncy breasts and buxom body complemented Sharon's tall and thin frame as their bodies entwined.

They were now writhing on the floor, kissing and stroking each other's bodies for pleasure, fondling and licking those areas they knew would bring them to orgasm. Sharon rolled onto her back, bringing her knees up. Andrea crawled to her aid. Lowering her head, she nestled her face in her friend's vagina. First, she just breathed deeply, long and hard, as Sharon began to respond. Andrea then began to lick and suck Sharon's sex. Michael took his cue...

Stripped naked and with a condom on, he got down on

his knees and entered Andrea's pussy from behind, bringing his right hand around to her front to stimulate her clitoris with his middle finger.

The threesome were each enjoying their arousal in different ways but the pleasure was the same. Michael's low grunts of satisfaction merged with the more audible exclamations from Andrea and Sharon. Three different voices harmonised into one sound which grew progressively more frenzied and loud.

Without warning Sharon let out a wail that signified she had reached her climax. It served as a trigger to Michael who could feel his seed about to shoot. Andrea begged him to hold on a moment longer. They ended up meeting each other half way as they came simultaneously. Michael gripped Andrea's hips and tensed as his seed flowed out of him.

For the next ten minutes a mess of tangled bodies lay on the lounge carpet trying to come back to earth. Michael's head spun in disbelief. He had never experienced group sex like this before. Nothing had matched this degree of lust and lack of inhibition. For all of them to come and at the same time was nothing short of amazing.

After a while they were all up and smoking spliffs, chilling out. As is the way with men, Michael and Alex said they were done for the evening, so the girls had to entertain themselves. Michael stretched out on the sofa while Alex sat in the armchair watching the two women orally excite each other in the '69' position, each one becoming a little more outrageous as the session went on.

The sound of Ragga FM eased Michael gently into Sunday morning. As his eyes focused, he tried to remember where he was. The surrounds of Andrea's bedroom started to become recognisable. He was naked and alone in her bed. In the bathroom next door, he could hear a shower running and downstairs he could just make out Alex's voice. The clock on the bedside table read 9:25.

"Bwoy, you look mash-up." Michael's first greeting of the day sounded off as he strolled into the lounge rubbing his eyes. Alex had been up a while and was sitting on the sofa reading a copy of Ebony magazine, a piece of toast in one hand.

Michael grunted and made his way into the kitchen where Andrea was making coffee.

"Wha'ppen baby," he said, holding her waist and kissing her on the neck.

From the lounge came Alex's voice.

"Rude bwoy listen up. I've persuaded the ladies that we should all go out for the day. Are you up for a run down to Brighton?"

Michael glanced out of the window. It was a bright sunny day. A cruise would be a good way to clear his head.

"Yeah, sweet. You gotta do the driving though, man."

Sharon returned from the bathroom and they all sat in the lounge eating breakfast and chatting. Despite having the discomfort of sharing the sofa with Sharon during the night, Alex seemed as fresh as a daisy and quite happy to gas away. The others — feeling in a more subdued mood — let Alex hold court with his stories. Alex was a natural comedian and could turn a story about going to buy a newspaper at the corner shop, into the funniest adventure. It was at times like this that Alex earned his keep. No matter how tired he or anyone else was, he saw it as his duty to keep an audience entertained. On a morning like this it was exactly what was needed to get everyone up and running.

They had left Hackney at about 10.45am and were now making good progress down the M3. In the back of Alex's Saab, Andrea and Michael relaxed in the deep tan leather seats watching the landscape go by. Up front, Alex was involved in a deep but good natured philosophical discussion about music.

"Cho'. He's a pussy."

Sharon was having none of it. "What d'ya mean 'pussy'?

He's kicking." She turned to Andrea for moral support.

"Andrea tell this fool that The Artist Formerly Known As Prince is the most talented man in the world."

Andrea was reluctant to get involved in this particular debate but felt she had to show sisterly solidarity.

"Don't bother with him, Sharon. Alex is one of them rough, common, unsophisticated dancehall bwoys."

"Who you calling bwoy?" It was said with just the right amount of mock indignation and timing.

The women fell about laughing and started Michael off as well. Alex grinned and kept his eyes on the road ahead.

The play fighting continued for the next half an hour until they reached the outskirts of Brighton, where Alex pulled in at a service station to get some petrol. While Alex went to pay, the others sat in the car and noticed the rather obvious looks they were getting from some of the other drivers.

"Check the bitch in the Volvo, she looks like she's expecting us to get our spears out."

Andrea and Sharon turned to stare back at the elderly woman giving them the eye. She quickly looked away.

Alex returned after a couple of minutes and climbed into the driver's seat. He too had noticed the reaction their presence was having on the other customers.

"It sure seems like the locals ain't too used to seeing niggas in these here parts," he said in a Deep South accent. Then flexing back to his normal south London voice, he added, loud enough for the occupants in the nearby cars to hear:

"It's the car. I get it all the time in this motor. They get pissed off seeing a black man driving a nice car. They're stuck in their nine to five jobs with family and mortgage and lickle mash up car. And they don't fucking like it. They figure you got it from drug dealing or some fuckries and they get vexed."

Reaching up to the top of the windscreen, Alex pulled back the two catches which secured the convertible hood to the screen.

As he pressed a switch on the centre console, the electric-powered hood folded backwards into a recess behind the rear passenger seats, filling the car with the warm sunlight.

"Now that should give them something to stare at."

Pulling the car away slowly, he looked to Sharon and pointed to the cassette player.

"Selector, come pump up the volume."

Ten minutes later they were cruising along Brighton seafront catching the sea breeze and enjoying the surprising warm sunshine. It was not a typical January day weather wise. The cries of seagulls and the splashing of the waves made this seaside town seem like a million miles away from the fume-filled and crowded streets of London. This was 100% pure chilling vibes.

They carried on along the seafront beyond Brighton, the Saab purring effortlessly in top gear and the wind clearing their minds. R. Kelly wafted out of the car's speakers and as they say, 'everyt'ing was copasetic'. They drove a few miles down the coast, before Alex did a U-turn and headed back toward town.

They stopped for lunch at Brighton's most expensive hotel, The Grand. As they sat tucking into their seafood dishes in the impressive glass-fronted Victoria Lounge, Alex recalled the hotel's only claim to fame. It was here at the 1984 Tory Party conference that the IRA blew up a large part of the building nearly killing Margaret Thatcher. He remembered the TV pictures of the time showing MPs and delegates being pulled from the rubble in their night clothes.

"Yeah man, you could see them coming out on stretchers in dem pyjamas. Some of them MPs must have been glad they weren't wearing dem ladies panty and suspender that night."

Even when discussing serious issues Alex couldn't resist throwing in a good measure of comic relief. The others laughed, but Sharon teased him all the same.

"Alex man, you're sick. You need help."

They sat and chatted for nearly two hours, enjoying the food, the good-natured company, and the dignified ambience of the restaurant. When the bill came Michael offered to settle it, but Alex snatched it back and said he'd deal with it. After some protest Michael conceded.

"It's cool. I have my flexible friend here." As ever he couldn't resist making a wisecrack.

"No Sharon, nah bother look down there," he said diverting his eyes to his groin. "When I said 'flexible friend' baby, I meant the card not that."

Michael and Andrea laughed, but Sharon pretended not to be amused. She eyed Alex with a mock look of disdain and spoke in an upper class English accent.

"I told you Alexander, darling, you're awfully sick. You really do need help."

The foursome spent the afternoon strolling along the beach with Alex picking Sharon up intermittently and threatening to throw her into the sea. They messed around on the pier and chanced their luck on jackpot machines in the amusement arcades. Michael challenged Alex to a race on the 'Le Mans' video car racing game and the two got into such a competitive spirit that the women finally had to drag them away. Six rounds of the game clearly weren't enough.

As it was starting to get dark, they found a seafront cafe where they ordered capuccinos and cheesecake. The conversation was animated and entertaining and they easily forgot the time. When she looked at her watch, Andrea was surprised that it was already 7.20pm. The hours had just flown by. As everybody was working the next day, they got themselves together to head back to London.

The steady stream of traffic on the M3 heading into London was an indication that a great number of the Capital's residents had decided to abandon the city for the weekend and head to the coast. In the crowded outside lane of the motorway, the Saab cruised at a steady eighty past a long, illuminated snake of traffic. Alex and Sharon were singing along to a classic Gwen Macrae tune:

You tried hard getting next to me.
I was so in love with you, I could hardly see.
Now it seems you wanna crawl back to me.
But after all this time, tell me can't you see,
All this love that I'm givin', givin' my love…

"Oh shit!"

They were singing so loudly, they barely heard Michael's exclamation.

"Shit," he repeated. "I should have been meeting a friend at Ronnie Scott's at eight. Fuck! I just forgot. All day and I now just remember. Cho'!"

"Just hope it's a good friend my man, 'cause that woman is gonna be well vexed wid you."

Michael knew that that was true. Monica was not the sort of woman you left standing in the cold with no excuse. But there was nothing he could do now. It was gone 8.00pm already. With this traffic, they would probably get back to Hackney in time to catch the National Anthem on the box.

He cursed himself and wondered what excuse he could come up with. All he knew was that he had to be totally convincing and totally sincere.

EIGHT

A loud round of applause almost obliterated his final words. A posse of black youths at the back of the assembly hall were particularly vociferous in their appreciation of his speech's sentiments. Raising their clenched fists in a circular motion they chanted a deafening, "booy, booy, booy!" sprinkled with loud whistles. Seated on wooden chairs at the front of the hall, the teachers smiled with some embarrassment at the raucous greeting their pupils had given the guest speaker.

As Michael walked off the stage and took his seat among the staff, the Headmaster patted his back by way of congratulation.

"Very good speech. I think you really got the message across", he said enthusiastically, pride beaming from his face.

Michael thanked him for his kind words, himself slightly surprised by the favourable reception he'd received.

St. Joseph's had changed quite a bit since Michael had been a pupil there. The depressing, red-brick Victorian structure of the main buildings was still intact, but the classrooms had a totally contrasting modern refit. The old whitewashed walls and graffiti etched wooden desks had been replaced by hi-tech grey walls and furniture more in keeping with a high street bank than a teenage institution of learning. Modern roller boards with wipeable felt pens had long taken over from the chalk and blackboards of his time. Computers that at one time were viewed with awe were now sprinkled liberally throughout the building.

To be walking the corridors of his old school was nothing short of momentous. Considering his conscientious efforts to shame its reputation, he was rather enjoying the irony of his return. A reformed bad boy speaking as a role model to others. The boy who knew the inside of the principal's office better than he knew his own front room, being hailed as a shining example of the virtues of capitalism and self-reliance! It seemed too strange to be true. But here he was, and from his reception, it seemed like the youngsters were grateful for his positive words about self-worth.

He didn't think the speech had been anything fancy, he'd just told it like it is. He started by telling them about his early clashes with authority and how he'd learned that you couldn't beat the system, you had to make it work for you. He stressed the need to believe in yourself no matter what others said and be proud of who you are.

The speech had come from the heart and was framed in language that the youths could relate to. It was important to him to relay these sentiments to the youngsters who seemed to be slipping into oblivion right before the community's eyes. Black or white, they could all understand where he was coming from and gave him maximum respect for that.

Two weeks ago when he had opened the letter, he was shocked to read that the Headmaster wanted him to come back to his old school in Brockley and give a 'careers' talk to the pupils. He had come to the conclusion that none of the old teachers could still be there, otherwise they certainly wouldn't be asking Michael Hughes to be any careers advisor. He was relieved to discover that he was right, and there had been a total change in staff over the years. The invitation had been the suggestion of one of the Governors who went to the same church as his mother.

As the late afternoon assembly broke up and the pupils prepared to head home for the day, members of staff once again congratulated and thanked him for taking the time out to talk to the pupils. As he strolled along past the trophy cabinet and Sports Noticeboard, memories of his days at St Joseph's came flooding back to him. He was no shining academic record, in fact he was lucky to have left with the meagre handful of O' levels and CSE's that he did. However, he did learn a lot about life at the school. His rudiments of maths didn't come from a textbook but from the hard world of playground bartering where goods were bought, sold and exchanged every day. His entrepreneurial skills didn't come from an economics class, but from his 'Rent-a-Razzle' empire, which he had pioneered in these very hallways. A wry smile crept across Michael's face. He wondered what his earliest anatomical volunteers were doing these days. Was Glenda Williams, who so kindly demonstrated the principals of head, 'head' of a large merchant bank? She said she wanted to work in a bank, so who knows. He chuckled at his own joke. And Valerie Hume, the girl whom he gave his virginity to, what became of her? Did she ever become the international singing sensation she was so sure she'd become? Or did she go and work in her mum's hair salon in New Cross, like he had predicted? Michael recollected the look of shock and disgust on old Mrs. Cranley's face, when he was caught in the sports equipment room with his dick in Glenda's mouth. The poor woman took them to the headmistress's office but was too embarrassed to tell her what she'd seen them doing. Faced with a lack of factual evidence the headmistress, Mrs Bailey, gave them a warning about being in a room unsupervised with 'dangerous sports equipment'.

Michael walked past the old headmistress's office. Mrs Bailey didn't deserve the title of 'Headmistress'. That rank belonged to Glenda, whose early mastery of oral sex made her truly the 'Mistress of Head'. Michael was enjoying this afternoon of meandering.

In the school car park, he saw a group of youngsters examining his BMW enthusiastically. Hot hands pressed against the glass, small fingers stroking the paintwork. De-badged, with lowered suspension, five spoke alloy wheels and small boot spoiler, the car stood out from the the regular BMW models. They smiled when Michael approached.

"Wicked car!" said one boy in a burgundy hooded coat.

Michael smiled and climbed into the cockpit.

"Now remember what I said in the assembly. Work hard, stay conscious, and believe in yourself. Then one day you'll all have cars much better than this one. Respek."

Michael pulled away and then stopped. Peering out of the driver's window, he turned his head back to the group.

"And another thing I forgot to tell you. Keep away from girls. Jus' go study yuh books. Yuh hear?"

The group threw their hands up in the air and shrieked in disbelief.

As he drove back to Blackheath, Michael tried phoning the number again. "No it's not urgent. Could you just tell her Michael Hughes phoned and I'll try her later. Bye."

He had been phoning Monica all day, but her secretary kept saying she was in one meeting or another. He couldn't tell if that was the truth or if she was deliberately avoiding his calls so he'd have to keep trying. Yes, he decided, she was avoiding him. He had phoned when he got in late the night before, only to talk to an answerphone. He did leave a message explaining how his friend's car had been involved in an accident in Brighton while they were visiting a client, and how it was impossible to get back to London in time. It was a plausible story he thought, but he figured she would still be annoyed. He knew it. He prided himself on his intuitive skills when it came to women, and having been involved with so many women, he believed he could read the signs and personality types inside out. His confidence often proved him right. Few women held surprises for him. He had spent most of his adult life in the pursuit of the female form, and learned something through every expedition. The elements that attract women to men were a constant study for Michael. What they want from a man and how a man could get what he wanted were also included in his subject list. The trick was being able to establish quickly what category a particular woman fell into. The mistake many men made was to assume that all women were impressed by the same things. The number of times he had overheard chat up lines where the guy was trying to impress with talk of his job title, his car and how much money he earned was astounding. The usual bullshit. What those guys didn't realise was that a lot of women just weren't interested in those 'attributes'.

Take the example of Sonia. She seemed to be the typical 'upwardly mobile' woman. He had tried all the good job, loadsamoney approach, but was getting nowhere. Later on, when he had all but given up trying to impress, he mentioned in passing that he helped out most weekends at a black Saturday school. She was so taken with his contribution to the community, that her whole attitude became much more welcoming.

Such was his reputation as an expert on women, that he would often be called upon by male friends as an advisor. During his Sunday football days, the members of the Simba Lions would seek out his opinion on both psychological and anatomical matters over lunchtime drinks. Michael took his 'advisor' role so seriously that on more than one occasion he consulted reference books for technical information and explanations. And like the car mechanic who is always asked for help from friends with their cars, Michael's assistance was requested on many sexual matters. His 'surgery' started in an informal light-hearted way, but developed to the point where his own curiosity became aroused and he was purchasing a number of books on the subject and truly becoming an expert.

It was always harmless good-natured banter with everyone taking the piss; but despite the humour they were all paying attention to what he had to say. No one would ever admit that a particular problem affected them. The questions were always veiled in the same language.

"Yeah Mikey, I read somewhere that…"

Or

"This mate had a girlfriend who liked…"

Or

"What do you reckon is the reason?"

The questions were as diverse as women themselves. For example, the question that Malcolm, the centre-half asked:

"Yeah Mikey, I was wid this girl the other night.Yeah? And she says that there is a big difference in the way man and woman have orgasm. Yeah? If, like a woman is turning a man on and he starts to come, if she stops dead he will still come. Yeah? But if you stop stimulating a woman as she has her first spasm, she won't carry on and come. You haffe carry on stimulating her for her to come. Is that right or is she just chatting doo-doo?"

Michael scratched his beard and pondered the question. For good measure he reached into his sports bag and retrieved a book. He scanned through the pages before giving his verdict in a mixture of upper class English judge and yardman talk.

"Well my good fellow, let me read what it says here:

'There is indeed a subtle difference in the sexual climax between male and female and also in its effect on each. Once the male climax has been reached and the reflexes activated, ejaculation will proceed automatically whether stimulation continues or not.

The situation in the female differs in two respects. First, the female has no ejaculatory apparatus and therefore no special muscles for this purpose. Instead, during orgasm and with continuing clitoral stimulation there occurs a rhythmic throbbing of the perineal muscles surrounding the vagina and urethra, and also a rhythmic contraction and relaxation of the muscles of the womb. These contractions are relatively weak compared with the powerful ejaculatory contractions of the male, and may continue for a somewhat longer period. So if clitoral stimulation ceases altogether immediately after climax is reached these rhythmic throbbings may cease and orgasmic sensation may not reach the same peak as if the stimulation had continued'. I hope that has answered your question. Next please."

Malcolm rubbed his chin, pondering the answer.

"Now, just run that through me again Supa."

Over the years, his library grew and he really did become something of an amateur sexpert. He had to begin stacking these books with the spine against the wall to disguise the sheer number. Like a man with any hobby, a trivial interest became a full blown obsession. He enjoyed knowing more about the infinite details of a woman's body than a woman and loved to see a woman's disbelief in meeting a man who knew so much. One girl was shocked and claimed it 'wasn't normal' for a man to know so much about the technical side of sex, but at the same time she was fascinated. Ultimately, it was a power trip to inform a woman about her sex and Michael particularly liked that feeling. Women would look at him as if he were an intruder, entering a realm exclusively for them. No matter how many women said they hated slack men, it was always that curiosity of a man knowing more and the essence of wickedness that dragged them towards the womaniser. His technical knowledge added to this sense of curiosity. Could this guy put into practice what he knew in theory? It was a question that many women wanted answering and Michael exploited that fact. Naturally.

The more of a dog he became, the easier it became to attract women. In his early days, he tried to hide his lifestyle to other potential partners. But he grew tired of playing the game and gave up the pretence. But it made no difference to his success rate. If anything it got better. His reputation spread and there was always another woman who had to discover for herself if this man really was as 'wicked in bed' as he professed to be.

He once bedded a woman from Harlesden, who admitted later that she wanted to sleep with him because her friend had described the 'mind-blowing' sex she had had with him. As in any 'profession', reputation is everything. A job well done gets referrals.

'Yeah, those Simba Lion counselling sessions had a lot to answer for', thought Michael.

Within a short time he was pulling up outside his Blackheath home, where for once he found a parking space. When he got inside, he pressed the 'Redial' button. Expecting to hear her secretary's voice, he was for a moment knocked off guard when Monica answered.

"Hello, Monica?"

"Yes, is this Mr. Hughes?"

"Oh, Monica if you only knew what happened to me last night. I am so sorry I didn't meet you at Ronnie Scotts. I am sincerely, sincerely, 'on my knees begging you please' sorry, but this is what happened: Myself and my spar Alex were on our way back from Brighton on the M3 — we were even early — behind this idiot in a mash-up Ford Capri, but for some reason he believed it was a Ferrari. Anyway, he was trying to race us, but we didn't pay no attention to the guy, well, he was so busy revving behind us then moving to our side, that he didn't see the roadworks fast approaching in front of him, so the only way he could get out of the situation was to ram the driver's side of our car. As he was going so fast, he took out the entire right side of Alex's Saab. Luckily for us a Police patrol car saw the whole incident, but we still had to spend hours hanging around making statements and arguing, with this idiot insisting we squeezed *him* out. Then on top of all that Alex had whiplash. It was an absolute nightmare — £900 worth of damage. Alex was so vex I thought he was gonna commit a homicide. So that's why I couldn't meet you. Monica…? Monica, are you still there?"

"Are you quite finished?"

Michael felt her chilled words bite. He knew he had laid it on a bit thick with his account of the events, but felt he was still convincing none the less.

"Ah, yes."

"That story is very interesting and I sympathise with your friend for losing half the wing of his car but that has nothing to do with me. Communication is such that I did not have to spend a second outside of Ronnie Scott's, let alone half an hour. I have a mobile, you have a mobile, use it. Don't waste my time, Michael, I don't appreciate it."

"I'm sorry." Michael was well and truly told off. He felt smaller than he'd felt in a very long time. Being disciplined by his Mum in Sunday school was his last recollection of being so belittled.

"I'm really sorry."

"Oh, for Christ's sake, stop saying you're sorry. It doesn't change anything."

"I suppose Friday night's out of the question?" He had to try and lighten the mood somehow. Getting another date was going to be difficult.

"I'm going to be a bit busy for the next few weeks, but I'll phone you when I'm less tied up."

He had used that line himself a million times; he knew exactly what it meant.

"Okay, Monica, I'm… I'll look forward to hearing from you. One last thing, don't hold this against me, otherwise the idiot in the Capri would have really won. Bye."

He knew how to counter attack and a tinge of guilt always fitted the bill.

He made a note in his diary to send Monica some flowers the next day with a card saying 'Give me a second chance'. Michael surprised himself. He sincerely wanted her to take his message to heart.

He went through his itinerary for the week checking on times for both business and social. He looked at Thursday and wondered if it was really worth taking the whole day off for the promotions day a publishing firm were organising. The problem was he might spend the best part of a day away from the office and end up with nothing to show for it. Too much of sales these days was speculative. You had to put yourself about and make contacts to obtain the long-term work, but there were usually no short-term gains to speak of. It was knowing whether to spend time, or not, courting a particular contact. That was 90% intuition, and Michael trusted his whole-heartedly. The computer market these days was so overloaded with players, that everyone was under mounting pressure.

He didn't mind pulling a few skanks to keep his edge over some of his competitors, but from the start of Mac In-Touch, he had decided that anything that was illegal was definitely out. He knew that lots of others were pulling scams, but he wasn't down with that. Even a lot of the supposed respectable dealers were at it.

One popular scam a few years ago, when the Apple Mac range was more limited and models had a longer production run life, was the 'old for new' con. Dealers would buy second-hand machines, often with damaged cases which knocked the price down. Then they would repackage the internal mechanisms in new cases and flog them off as brand new machines. Or sometimes as a quick hit, you could package a low grade machine in the case of a more expensive one and sell it as the bonafide item. By the time the unsuspecting purchaser had realised that his machine was no more powerful than the old one, the seller had disappeared. These days the big trade was in outright theft and many machines were shipped abroad.

Michael and Josey took particular care about who they bought second-hand machines from and tended to just deal with regular and trusted contacts. They were fully aware of the prejudices in society, and as a black-owned business they were often viewed with suspicion by potential clients, so they could not afford to be anything but legit.

Michael had arranged to meet up with Barbara that evening so he had a shower and ironed a white linen shirt. He had some time to spare so he finished off a proposal for a new system for the PR department of an American bank in the City. It was hardly worth the paperwork in terms of income generated, but at least it was turnover.

Barbara was the sort of woman who liked to look after her man. Tonight she had made an extra special effort to make sure everything was going to be perfect for their evening together. Knowing his passion for seafood, she had prepared a New Orleans seafood gumbo, brimming with crab, lobster, Tiger prawns and cod chunks served with saffron rice and a variety of carefully prepared vegetables. For desert, a chocolate meringue, strawberry and cream gateau awaited their attention in the fridge.

She was in her element in the kitchen and loved cooking, especially for others. She would happily have cooked everyday if there was a man around the house to please. While other women craved independence and careers, Barbara would be the first to admit, that all she wanted out of life was to have a nice home, a husband and kids. That was the type of stability she had never had as a child, and now as an adult it was all she wanted. Her parents had divorced when she was seven and her mother died two years later. She grew up with an aunt she had never met before the tragedy and she would barely be able to recognise her father today.

In contrast, Michael had known stability all his life. His parents were still happily married, 35 years on, still living in the Brockley house he had grown up in. While they had never been wealthy, he hadn't grown up with some of the financial hardships that many of his peers knew too well.

Barbara had even gone to the hairdresser that afternoon so she could look her best. It had meant taking time off work, but she so wanted the evening to go well that it seemed a small sacrifice to make. She was concerned that the mood between them had deteriorated since their last meeting at the Chinese restaurant. Tonight she wanted it to be a special night to remember. She had even bought some new Victoria's Secret underwear at the weekend, with the evening in mind.

Michael was oblivious to the fact that Barbara had long known that he was seeing other women. As long as Michael kept the details away from her, she felt he had fulfilled his role sufficiently. He made time for her, she was happy; if she did not hassle him about who he saw when they weren't together, so was he.

As she gave the scarlet sauce a stir for the final time, the doorbell rang. Eight o'clock on the dot. Barbara was surprised that for once Michael was on time. He greeted her with a hug and a bunch of roses and stepped into the flat which oozed with the intoxicating scent of herbs, spices and Barbara. She quickly twirled around to exaggerate the motion of her black chiffon dress, as she looked for a vase. Michael relaxed in the front room.

"What, didn't you pay the electric bill?" he jokily commented referring to the number of candles burning in the house.

She returned from the kitchen with a disappointed expression and placed the vase of flowers on the pine dining table at the other end of the long lounge.

"This evening I thought we should dine by candlelight. All electric lights are banned," she informed him as the orange glow filled the room.

"I was only jesting. It all looks nice."

Barbara's face brightened.

Michael sat at the table opening a bottle of chilled champagne, as Barbara brought in the last of the small bowls of vegetables.

"Wow. Me nevah know it was my birt'day. You certainly know how to make a man feel good, Barbara."

"Thanks, Michael," she said proudly.

"Yeah. I've always said you'll make someone a good wife one day."

Barbara smiled. Michael quickly realised the mistake in mentioning the word 'wife'.

"The problem is finding the right man. They seem in such short supply," she said.

"I'm sure if you keep looking you'll find him."

Hopefully, the mistake was rectified.

"I think I already have . He just needs a little time to recognise a good thing when he sees it."

Maybe not.

The verbal duelling had been good-natured, but suddenly the mood changed with her last remark. Michael's smile disappeared from his face and he began to examine every grain of rice on his plate.

Barbara chose not to notice the change and continued.

"What can a girl do when she's madly in love with a guy and just wants to have his children?" She said it as a joke, but 'many a truth is spoken in jest'.

Michael was transfixed by the skin on one of his prawns. The deafening silence made her regret her admission.

Suddenly, Michael broke the deadlock. Laying his fork on the plate, he looked her straight in the eye.

"I gotta tell you something, Barbara. I think things have

run their course with us, I mean with this relationship."

He continued in a solemn precise manner. As he spoke his gaze drifted downwards to the table.

"Things have become a bit too intense, if you know what I mean? I ain't really looking for no serious relationship right now, and I think you want something else. You understand? It's not that I don't feel for you, I just don't want it to run like this."

"What are you saying Michael?" Her hand reached up to cover her mouth.

"Well it's not really gonna happen between us is it? You know what I mean? I think it's time to knock it on the head. I mean, end the relationship. It done, it finish."

He scratched his hair and shuffled uneasily in his chair. A gloss came over Barbara's eyes, she couldn't let this man just walk out of her life like this. She had to do all she could to rectify the situation.

"Michael, if there's something I'm doing to annoy you just let me know and I'll try and change it. If I'm not giving you enough space just tell me. Please Michael, just tell me."

With every word she uttered, her voice became more uncertain and less able to camouflage the desperation that loomed in her soul. Her palms turned to the heavens to push home her point.

It was the sort of ending all men hated. Michael was no exception. He would rather a woman who cursed you or cuts up your best clothes, but not a pleader. An uncomfortable feeling of guilt and hatred filled him. *Does the bitch not have any self-respect? How could she beg in such an undignified way? Why was she doing it? Why did I allow the situation to develop? Oh shit, suppose she does something silly? But she wouldn't… Would she?*

He felt like an executioner. As the victim is led to the scaffold he starts to struggle and starts pleading for his life. The executioner knows he must do his job. He feels guilty for taking the man's life but, at the same time, he hates the man for making him feel this guilt.

"Barbara, it's nothing to do with you. I just don't want to

be involved with anyone."

The surprise of his statement combined with her high expectations for the evening proved too much to handle. She tried to contain herself, but to little effect.

Tears flowed down her face and dripped onto her plate. Michael blew a fuse.

"What you giving me all this shit for? Jeezus Chris' what's your fucking problem? I never promised you a rahtid t'ing. I never said I was going to settle down with you or anything. Just get the fuck off my back."

His chair flew back and startled Barbara into silence. Throwing his napkin onto the table, he was on his feet. His outburst had come to an end so a quick exit was in order. Barbara began to rise, wiping the tears from her face and correcting her hair. She looked him dead in the eye with a kind of conviction which he had not seen from her before. As he walked past her, she followed his every step. Even when he couldn't see her face, he knew that her stare was piercing his body. He fetched his jacket from the sofa, and made one final look back to see Barbara slowly shaking her head, her dress clenched in one hand. He slammed the front door hard behind him.

He floored the car's accelerator and screeched away from Barbara's flat. He didn't want to think about what had happened or how he had reacted. He channelled his aggression on the road ahead and drove like a maniac. Pounding the steering wheel, he was cutting up other drivers, overtaking and jumping red lights. A near crash at a junction eventually brought him round to his senses and he slowed down to a degree of sanity.

Shortly after, he was pulling up outside his house. He locked the car, opened his front door and let a large spliff wipe the evening from his memory.

Barbara, took the pot of seafood gumbo and poured it into the bin, over her photo of Michael.

NINE

The detective constable ran his finger along the columns of figures, trying to find a match between the list of stolen machine ID numbers and the computer in front of him. Unsuccessful, he moved to another machine and repeated the procedure. His colleague was examining a pile of invoices and receipts. The other two uniformed officers milled around opening cupboards and drawers, but they seemed uncertain as to what exactly they were looking for.

Michael sat on his desk with a look of frustration and disgust on his face.

"Look, officer, if you told me what this was all about maybe I could help you."

The stockier one going through the invoices looked up.

"As I told you earlier when I showed you the warrant, Sir, we have reason to believe that we may find stolen computer equipment located on these premises."

"Listen don't talk to me like I'm an idiot. You said that bollocks before. What I'm saying, is why do you think there is stolen equipment *here*?"

Michael was getting vexed and it was annoying the officer, who was trying to do it by the book.

"I'm not treating you like an idiot, Sir. I am not at liberty to disclose that information. I have a warrant to conduct this search and the sooner I can get this done, the sooner I can leave. Your cooperation is appreciated." It was said with the same delivery as a British Rail announcer. Michael could see he was wasting his time.

Josey, was standing observing the proceedings and spinning two metal balls in his palms. He stood by the entrance to the back office and reassured his brother.

"Don't worry about it, Mikey. Let them look all they want cause they ain't gonna find nothing dodgy here."

Michael kissed his teeth, knowing that what his brother had said was true.

Josey motioned to Cynthia to carry on with her work. She tried to ignore what was going on.

After an hour's sifting and rummaging, the officers left empty-handed and obviously disappointed.

Once the officers had gone, the brothers began the post-mortem.

"It's someone setting us up. It was a tip-off that got them down here. Why else come now, on the off chance? We've been here for nearly two years."

Michael's prognosis sounded about right.

"Yes, boss. That seems about de size ah dat," was Josey's verdict. He went a step further. "I have my suspicions that those people from Micro Chippie done it. They'd have to be stupid if they couldn't guess that we skanked them with the Russians."

"Joseph, if I find out it was those pussies, I'm gonna get 'nuff rude bwoy to go up there and cut their raas."

"Don't bother with that kind of foolishness. We just have to watch our backs. Anyway I've got work to do."

With that Josey disappeared into the back office and got on with his day.

Michael had just started to straighten out some of the disruption made to the office by the boys in blue, when Cynthia's shriek almost made him jump.

"It's him, It's him. Nah man, it can't be. It is. He's coming in here!"

The shop door opened and in stepped a short, dark-skinned youth with a green and orange ragga suit. He was adorned with copious amounts of gold jewellery and some devilish gold darkers. In one hand, he carried a mobile in a suede case and in the other a black laptop computer. He was no more than 19, but carried himself with the confidence of someone older.

The youth pushed his shades down his nose and nodded a greeting to Cynthia who couldn't contain herself.

"You're Maxi Fabulous aren't you?" she gushed.

The yout' smiled and rested his gold ringed fingers on his chest.

"Well, it no lie. 'Tis I, you spy. I don't mean to brag, I don't mean to boast. But Fabulous is the one the girls like most. I don't leave it to chance, I don't leave it to luck. If de gal is willing, I'm able to…"

"Can I help you?" Michael's interjection halted the romeo rapper in mid-sentence.

"Yes, boss. I need a printer lead for dis yah t'ing," he said handing over the laptop.

In the last six months the young and outrageous Maxi Fabulous had risen from obscurity to number 1 in the reggae charts. Every other tune on the pirates these days seemed to be either a Maxi song, re-mix or cover version. Maxi's potent musical brew of ragga, jungle and slack soul was proving an addictive cocktail for female music lovers the length and breadth of the nation. With killer tunes like *'Jungle Heat'*, *'Rough Rider'* and *'Hot Spot'* burning up the dancehall, Maxi was living large and enjoying the ride.

Michael, while not being a big fan of Maxi's furious tunes, had 'nuff respect for the yout' who had pioneered a new sound and was carving a career in a field he clearly loved.

Michael complimented the youth on his recent success and went back to locate a cable. When he returned, Maxi was eyeing one of the newest Power Mac models with interest.

"Yeah. I hear these are wicked machines. But you need the right version software."

Maxi obviously knew his Apples from his pears. Michael was impressed and for the next half hour the two got deeply engrossed in a discussion about the latest developments in the world of Apple computing. Maxi was so pleased with the chat that he decided there and then that he must have a Power Mac. He reached into his pocket and pulled out a silver money clip rammed with £50 notes. After a bit of haggling, Michael agreed on a price and the deal was done. Maxi was happy with his computer and Michael was well chuffed at selling £1400 worth of hardware.

Helping Maxi load the computer box into the star's Mercedes, Michael passed Maxi his card and told him that if there was anything he could do for him, he should give him a bell.

"Well boss", thought Maxi, "there is a lickle favour you could do fe we. I don't like joke, I don't like to jest. But when…"

Michael cut him short.

"Maxi, man jus' come tell me what you want."

"Well just pass this to the daughter in there fe we."

Maxi handed Michael his card and smiled to Cynthia who was oggling the ragga star through the Mac In-Touch's main display window.

Michael smiled and took the card.

"Supa, it will be my pleasure. Respek."

The Kilburn McDonald's was in its usual lunchtime state of frenzy. Long queues of hungry customers waited impatiently to be served as the staff raced frantically to get the orders processed as quickly as possible. Navigating his tray through the crowds, Michael spotted an empty table near the front window. It was a relief to have finally been served and it was a relief to be able to take a break away from the office. He unpackaged his food and started to munch reflectively on his McChicken sandwich. He didn't want to think about it, but his mind started running through the events of the previous night. He was a little surprised that Barbara had not phoned him when he got in. Knowing Barbara's style he had expected her to call and apologise. He wondered what she was thinking and feeling this morning. Was she really pissed off? Was she hurt? Was she embarrassed? *Ah, she'll get over it in a couple of weeks*, he thought.

His attention focused on the young black guy in the leather jacket sitting at the table opposite. The youth seemed to be about 18 years old, but his face looked as if it carried the responsibilities of a man older than his teenage years. His girlfriend, who looked of a similar age, had just got up and was putting a baby into a push chair. The youth wearily finished his drink and got up to help his woman. The look on the youngster's face haunted Michael. From the unpleasantness with Barbara, his mind now started to reflect on the situation with Jackie. Was she really pregnant? How would he deal with it if she was? He had avoided being a baby father for so many years and it seemed almost inconceivable that it would happen at this stage in his life. Some day, he wanted to have children, but it would be with the woman he married, he had always told himself. This situation with Jackie really didn't fit into his life plan. He wanted to phone her and find out if there was any news, but he felt that it would be tempting fate. He would rather wait until she told him. The longer time went on the greater the likelihood that things would be all right. Logic went out of the window at these times.

While in a morose mood anyway, he decided he might as well run through the whole range of problems awaiting him. He didn't need to give any time to the ongoing financial difficulties, he had already allocated enough reflection to that on his morning drive into work. The situation with Shantelle, like the one with Barbara required some attention. She had phoned him a number of times over the last few weeks, but fortunately for Michael she had only been able to speak to his answerphone. He had hoped that not returning her calls would have given her a clear message. This lack of response only seemed to encourage her however, and the frequency of her calls had reached menacing proportions. He was grateful he'd not given her his mobile number for that would have robbed him of any escape.

He'd met the bubbly Shantelle at a West End night club just over a year ago. It was lust at first sight for both of them and what seemed as though it was going to be a one night fling, had developed into something more. They carried on seeing each other and gradually Shantelle got more into him. For Michael's part his interest was largely physical, but not just in the sexual sense. Shantelle had been blessed with the sort of body and face that most women would have died for. She was the closest to Michael's image of perfect black beauty and Michael enjoyed the envious looks other guys gave him when he was out with her. As is often the case with many beautiful women, Shantelle had been able to get through life relying on her good looks, so she did not feel the need to develop her mind or personality. She grew up being told she could marry any man she wanted because of her looks. She believed it totally, until she got into her twenties, and noticed the list of ex-boyfriends starting to grow. She had no problem attracting guys, but the type she wanted, didn't stick around for too long.

Michael was like those other disappearing ex's. He liked her looks and thought she was okay to be with, but her lack of intellect and spiritual depth, meant she could only ever be a passing bit of amusement.

At times he was surprised at how long it had lasted, but the ego trip of a beautiful women on his arm was a strong incentive to keep things going. But every ego trip has its final destination, and Michael reckoned he'd now come to the end of this particular journey. He'd grown tired of the lack of interesting conversation when they were out together, and he was weary of being her teacher. At twenty six, he believed she was too old for him to be telling her that Picasso was a painter, or that Luxembourg was in Europe. He didn't want to be her life's guide, always teaching and showing, but getting nothing in return.

He had made the mistake of spending too much time with her and getting sucked into the egotistical indulgence of female beauty. Shantelle's pride would never allow her to play second fiddle to another woman, so she would not have tolerated Michael openly dating others. He'd seen that in her personality from the start and had made the decision to lie to her about his countless other intimate encounters. It seemed the easy option at first, but it was now the rod she used to beat him with. He had made his bed, but now he realised that he wasn't feeling sleepy at all.

Shantelle's departure would be very different from Barbara's; he could see that. While Shantelle was equally happy to pledge her undying love for Michael, she was also a woman with a strong measure of pride and a vengeful heart.

'Hell hath no fury like a woman scorned', and he shuddered at the thought of the fury Shantelle could inflict on him. He'd already had a glimpse of the potential volcano that lay below her seemingly gracious exterior and it worried him.

The incident six months ago was still etched in his memory. It was in an East London night club and one of Michael's slightly intoxicated ex-lovers formed the backdrop to a night he would not forget in a hurry. It was that old cliché of girlfriend going to toilet and returning to find ex-lover holding on to boyfriend, whispering sweet nothings in his ear. After Shantelle had laid out cold the unfortunate girl with a well-aimed right hook, she proceeded to attack Michael with fingernails blazing, her face contorted to show a less attractive aspect — a rage that seemed beyond her small frame. It required the strength of three burly bouncers to hold back the female typhoon.

Unlike Barbara, there was going to be no final showdown in the relationship with Shantelle, Michael had long decided. It had to fade away, gently. It would require some ducking and diving, he calculated, but he reckoned a policy of conflict avoidance would illicit the desired long term effect. He knew it would be a prolonged struggle as persistence was one of Shantelle's fortes. But could he get away with it? That was the question he didn't have the answer to.

He got home at about 9.00pm that evening. The time wasted with the cops had to be made up so it had meant spending a few extra hours in the office. After preparing a bland TV dinner in the microwave, he sat down in the lounge and played his answerphone messages back.

"Hi Michael how ya doing? This is Cheridah here calling from

Washington just to touch base and say a belated Happy New Year. Hope my big fella is taking care of himself and staying out of mischief. Speak to you real soon and have a nice week. Bye."

"Yes, rude bwoy. Jus' to tell you I'm having a road block session at my yard this Saturday night. There's going to be 'nuff pretty gal down here so jus' mek sure you bring yuhself. Oh… and a bottle. Lickle more… Oh yeah, it's Herbie speaking."

"Hello Michael. I'm starting to think that you're avoiding me. I know you're busy, but please could you get back to me. The time of the call is 8.15, my name is Shantelle Cleveland and I think you know my number. Goodbye."

"Hello, darling, its your Momma. You know I hate dis chupid machines. Just callin' to fin' out how you keepin' and remember it's your Papa birt'day next week. Love you… an' what I do now…? Jus' put it down? Okay."

"Hello Michael, it's Monica here. Thanks for the flowers they are gorgeous. You're still not in my Good Books, but you're now out of my Bad Books. Keep working at it. Take care and speak to you soon."

"Look Michael, I'm really sorry about last night. I'm sorry if I've been pressuring you. If you're free at the weekend it would be good to see you. Nothing heavy, just as friends. Let me know, Okay? Bye."

Michael stopped eating and slid the plastic tray onto the coffee table. It was hardly the tastiest of meals to start with, and now he'd lost his appetite all together. Even in his own yard he was not free from the hassles. At least he heard his mother's voice. It was always hard to find quality time to spend with his parents, but he knew he had to make the effort. He played her message back again and laughed. His parents were inseparable, even during a phone message.

She had to have her 'Dumpling' by her side, his father's mumblings towards the end were clear enough. Would he ever find companionship like that? The kind that would last 35 years? He knew none of the women who left him messages that day could be 'the one'. Why couldn't those witches leave him alone? There were plenty of men out there; why did they have to come and harass him? Sometimes he wondered if he was getting too old to play the man about town but what were the alternatives? He liked his freedom and women too much for him to take up the restrictive, suffocating life of monogamy. Just the sound of the word made him feel depressed. Monogamy. Was it such a coincidence it sounded so much like monotony? No, the two were as linked as rice and peas, he reckoned. And he didn't like the sound of either, not at this moment anyhow. 'Sure, I'll get married one day', he told himself. 'But if you know the right woman hasn't come along, why go through a whole dress rehearsal with someone who ain't gonna be on stage with you at the play's opening night?' That was the argument and it seemed to make a whole heap of sense to him.

If he needed to convince anyone further about the validity of his position he only would tell them he was a Sagittarian. Sagittarian are ill suited to a one to one relationship and craved the independence and freedom that comes from playing the field. Life was not about nibbling on one cherry, it was about tasting the whole bowl. He argued that he was a victim of astrological circumstance, and so there was nothing he could do about it. It wasn't an argument that Michael totally believed, but when a woman was putting him under fire, it was a convenient bullet proof jacket to reach for.

Michael pondered his fate for a moment more.

"Cho'!" He told himself. "This is pure foolishness."

He picked up the phone and dialled Monica's mobile.

She sounded mellow and relaxed and not unhappy to hear his voice.

"Listen Monica I know you said you were a bit busy at

the moment, but if you're free on Friday night I would really enjoy taking you to dinner."

"I am actually free on Friday, because of a cancellation, but I don't want any confusion. I'm not a teenager who is just going to hang around waiting."

"Monica, I know you're still pissed off at me but I'm going to make it up to you on Friday. My honour is at stake here."

Monica had to laugh at Michael's exaggeration, and he arranged to pick her up at her office after work at 7.00pm. She did add one proviso:

"You're going to have to work hard for me, Michael."

He reclined back on the sofa with a smile on his face.

Anything worth having is worth working for.

TEN

The Saab was approaching the right-hand corner far too quickly. As the driver realised his mistake he tried to compensate by applying firmer pressure on the brakes. He calculated incorrectly, locking the rear wheels with a huge plume of white smoke. The car lurched to the left, then quickly went into a rapid spin that hurtled it off the tarmac into a grassy bank. The other cars following quickly on the Saab's tail only just managed to get round the corner without making contact.

"Bad luck."

Rupert DeBorchgrave shouted his condolences and lowered his binoculars. Casually dressed in jeans and a red Ferrari paddock jacket, the middle-aged aristocratic publisher was obviously enjoying himself. He smiled and shook his head in disbelief.

"Not enough opposite lock," he informed the gathered party.

Brands Hatch was the venue for the seventh round of the British Saloon Racing Championship. The bright sunlight was making the meeting a pleasant spectator event, despite the chilly weather.

The race was an ideal opportunity for the millionaire publisher to entertain staff, clients and others in the trade. Michael had come along as the guest of Tony Batson, the ad manager of one of DeBorchgrave's consumer magazines. He'd known Tony for a few years and they both shared a passion for cars.

A large hospitality marquee had been set up for the two hundred guests and food and drink was in plentiful supply. It was an ideal opportunity for Michael to network and make some contacts in the publishing world where Apple Macs were standard equipment. He had come prepared with a box of business cards and had spent the morning circulating and striking up conversations with the various guests. It had all gone well and there were several leads for him to follow up at a later date. All he needed now was the chance to introduce himself to DeBorchgrave, but this was easier said than done. The publisher was constantly surrounded by a large group of admirers, all vying for his attention.

He decided to wait until after lunch to try and make contact. In the meantime, he'd check out the machinery parked up in the paddock. In between the various racing car transporters and mechanic's equipment vehicles, there was an impressive number of exotic road cars. He stopped to admire a brand new Ferrari F355 sports car. Michael had read a lot about this new supercar which was being hailed as the finest Ferrari ever built. The stunning red two-seater with its high performance V8 engine was the ultimate in current road going technology and at £85,000 it was very much a rich man's plaything. Michael followed the graceful lines of the vehicle and pondered just how many women's necks would turn on seeing him behind the wheel of such a superior vehicle.

"Fancy a spin."

Michael turned to see a smiling Rupert DeBorchgrave walking towards the car. The publisher offered his hand.

"Rupert DeBorchgrave. Saw your face earlier on with Tony. Sorry we've not had the chance to meet."

"You are not the easiest man to gain access to," Michael said, introducing himself and handing DeBorchgrave a card.

"I was just getting some papers from the car. I picked her up yesterday and any excuse I can get to take her out on the road is wonderful. So, do you fancy a quick spin?"

"Mr. DeBorchgrave, I'm ready when you are."

"No please, call me Rupert."

Michael sank into the luscious seats, the rich smell of leather filling his nostrils. The vehicle smelt of success. DeBorchgrave started up the car and the engine roared into life. Pulling out of the paddock, Rupert gunned the engine and the car shot down the exit road and out of Brands Hatch into the Kent countryside. The performance and handling of the Ferrari was breathtaking. He would rapidly approach a fast moving car from behind, and when the slightest gap appeared, he would slip the chromed gear lever down a notch and stomp on the accelerator. The Ferrari overtook the other vehicle at an unbelievable rate of knots before zipping back into lane. The sensation pushed Michael's body further back into the seats.

In between the deafening scream of the engine as the revs rose, Michael sang the car's praises and told DeBorchgrave his line of work.

"I tell you what Michael, see my wife Trudi; she'll be along later this afternoon. She's the editor on one of my titles, New Interiors. They need all their systems updating and they are going to need quotes. I'll introduce you when she gets here. Good gracious, look at the time, we have to start making our way back. Our fun is over I'm afraid."

He reluctantly turned the car round and headed back to Brands Hatch.

As they pulled up in the paddock a number of the guests were waiting to speak to DeBorchgrave. Several of them were astonished to see Michael climbing out of the Ferrari. Everyone was vying to get the old man's attention and they wondered how this 'darkie' had not only accomplished this, but been given special treatment. In the small-minded male world of corporate advancement, seemingly petty things took on a major significance.

As Michael strolled back to the marquee he recognised the Micro Chippie salesman from the airport. DeBorchgrave made the introduction.

"Martin, let me introduce you to one of your rivals. This is Michael Hughes from Mac In-Touch." DeBorchgrave turned to Michael. "Martin works for Micro Chippie."

The Micro Chippie man reluctantly shook his rival's hand and tried to stick the knife in with the other.

"Mac In-Touch? Gosh, I thought the police closed you lot down ages ago."

Michael took the comment in his stride.

"You must be confusing us with another firm. We are very much alive and doing everything by the book."

DeBorchgrave laughed.

"As far as I'm concerned if one's not had a few visits from the Old Bill, one's running their business a bit too carefully for my liking. I'd be embarrassed to tell you how many times the Serious Fraud Squad have visited my businesses."

Everyone joined in the laughter, but no one was too sure whether it was a joke or if he truly meant it.

Lunch was being served as the group returned to the marquee where Michael caught up with his spar, Tony.

"What's going down, Tone?"

A tall balding guy in his mid-thirties with a small moustache, Tony nodded and waited until he had finished his mouthful of food.

"Oh nothing much. Just getting some nosh while it's going. That's the only point with these hospitality beanos. It's how much food and drink you can get and how much time you can wangle out of the office," said Tony, in his cultured cockney accent.

"Yeah and some nice women wouldn't go amiss. They seem in short supply round here," added Michael.

"Well, that sort of thing doesn't interest me any more. In four weeks time, I'm kissing my bachelor days goodbye."

"Lawd, another member of the Rude Boys Club hands in his membership card. I think you're mad," joked Michael, "but congratulations anyway." He shook hands with his friend enthusiastically. "So who's the unlucky girl then? Some blind woman with a history of mental illness in her family?"

"Oi! Leave it out. I'm a bloody eligible catch I am. Upwardly mobile thirtysomething buppy, mate," Tony added. "Come along to the wedding and you'll find out who she is. She's one of the few women in London who's escaped your nasty clutches, or should that be crotches?"

Tony explained that he and his girlfriend had only decided in the last few days to tie the knot. They didn't want a fussy wedding so were getting married quietly at the local town hall in Harlow, Essex, where he lived. They were going to have a small reception in a hotel nearby for the sixty or so invited guests.

"I'll be sending out the invites in the next week or so, so make sure I see your mug," he told Michael.

The two buddies stood chatting about the 'old days', cars, publishing and computers for the next half-hour. The other guests were progressively becoming louder and more intoxicated, as the waiters dispensed the complimentary wine. A courtesy coach, which had collected the majority of the guests, would be dropping them back in London. As a result, they saw the event as an ideal opportunity to get well pissed. Michael felt a presence behind him.

"Michael, let me introduce my wife Trudi to you."

Michael recognised DeBorchgrave's pronounced upper class accent. He turned and tried to maintain his composure. He recognised her at once, but her lack of expression made him question his judgement. He looked again. It couldn't possibly be her. The bounce of her blonde hair confirmed it. The same woman that he had so vigorously sexed at Heathrow airport stood before him.

"It's a pleasure to meet you." The woman shook his hand and looked him straight in the eye. She spoke in such a relaxed manner about the magazine and their computer system that after a while, Michael began to doubt that it was the same woman. No, he must have made a mistake; no one could have played it that cool, could they?

Deborchgrave returned to his wife and handed her a glass of Champagne and cassis.

"Michael, I wonder if we may have the pleasure of your company this evening for dinner at our house? I thought it would be the ideal opportunity to sort out the equipment deal. I live just outside Sevenoaks which is about 20 minutes drive from here. Afterwards my driver can drop you back to London," said the publisher.

Tony choked. Michael couldn't believe his luck and accepted the offer.

"Splendid, we'll see you after the last race." The Deborchgraves made their excuses and departed, leaving Tony still agog with disbelief.

"Bloody hell, how d'ya get that? I've worked there four years and I'm lucky if the pussy says 'good morning'."

Michael adjusted his tie and smiled.

"When you know how to be enthusiastic about a customer's passions, you're gonna land the sale."

"Eh?" asked a puzzled Tony.

"Start chat about Ferraris next time you see him, Supa."

This was truly a miraculous day. Not only was he spending the evening with one of the most important figures in British magazine publishing, but he was behind the wheel of an 85 grand Ferrari blasting down the M25. Next to him sat DeBorchgrave's wife. The publisher had taken his wife's Mercedes, so he could drop off a few friends before returning to his home. Michael was left with the pleasure of driving his wife home in a Ferrari. At this point, the experience of driving a Ferrari far exceeded the company. Mrs. DeBorchgrave was silent.

The Italian sportscar was a dream. If there was ever an incentive to work to become a millionaire, this car was it. As he turned off the motorway and eventually into Sevenoaks every head in the town turned, mouths opened wide, looking at this black guy in a flash car. He probably would have got the same looks in downtown Brixton, so it didn't bother him too much. In fact he rather liked the feeling, especially as so many of those faces looked pissed off.

They drove for a few miles out of Sevenoaks until Trudi gestured for him to turn down a small country lane. They then made a bend into another smaller track and then eventually turned into the gravel drive of an imposing, white-fronted Georgian country house. They parked outside the front door, then entered the house.

The DeBorchgraves knew how to live in style. A beautiful marble floored hall laden with antiques provided a circular focus to the house. The atrium had a domed ceiling, exquisitely painted, and a number of rooms leading from the hall.

Trudi showed Michael into the sitting room and offered him tea, then she disappeared to the kitchen. He relaxed in one of the large settees in the room, admiring the antique music box on the side table. The whole house had been tastefully restored in traditional Georgian style. All the detailing was correct down to the furniture and paintings on the walls. It had the kind of sophistication that Michael aspired to.

Trudi arrived shortly with a silver tea service on a tray. She poured him a cup, offering him him the sugar to add to his own taste. It was all very stiff, English and polite. Michael listened to the woman talking about what needed doing around the garden at this time of year. He still felt embarrassed for thinking it was the same woman at the airport. He heard white people saying of black people 'that they all look alike'. Maybe it was his turn.

They chatted away politely for the next hour until Rupert DeBorchgrave returned home. While he entertained Michael in his study, Trudi went to prepare the dinner in the kitchen. The study housed an impressive amount of automotive memorabilia from the start of the century. Cars were among DeBorchgrave's great passions. He owned a 1962 Jaguar 'E' type roadster, a 1972 Ferrari Daytona, and a 1969 Lamborghini Muira which were housed in garages at the back of the house. He suggested that if Michael was interested they could go and pay the cars a visit after dinner.

The study also contained some impressive computer technology, which contrasted with the period decor. DeBorchgrave had a fax within his Apple Mac and scanner set up in the room so that at anytime he could receive page proofs or covers directly on screen for approval. Life could be so easy when you had the money. If he had this set up in his pad in Blackheath, he would hardly need to go into the office, thought Michael.

By most people's standards, Michael was living the good life, with his nice house in Blackheath and his BMW. But everything was relative. No matter how well off you were, there was always some guy who was living larger than you.

He could never accept that he had reached the top, there is no such thing. Now that he had seen how the other half lived, Michael realised that this was the sort of wealth he wanted and deserved to have.

Trudi appeared at the study door and informed the men that dinner was ready in the dining room.

Michael was somewhat disappointed with the meal; he had been expecting some lavish dish to go with the setting of the house. But instead he tucked into a rather rough piece of steak with an assortment of over-cooked vegetables. His mind wandered briefly back to Barbara's impressive meal on the Monday night and he was pleased to think that when it came to cooking, the rich didn't always get the best.

Michael looked at his watch and saw it was gone 8.20pm. He had better start discussing what system Trudi's company required, he thought. He really didn't want to go away without something fairly definite being agreed in regards to a sale.

"So Trudi, what machines were you thinking of upgrading to?"

DeBorchgrave politely but swiftly cut him short.

"Michael, no offence old chap, but there is a rule in this house. We never discuss business over dinner. It gives Trudi such bad indigestion that we've put a ban on it. After dinner when we're relaxing is fine."

"No problem. It's the salesman in me; I always want to talk business. Apologies. After dinner is fine", Michael agreed.

After a few glasses of brandy the DeBorchgraves showed their guest into the lounge where a fire was already burning in the hearth. A couple of small table lamps illuminated the room which was bathed in the warm light from the fire. Trudi poured their guest another large glass of brandy.

Rupert sat down with his wife on the sofa, fiddling with a leather riding crop which had been lying idle on a side table next to a show jumping riding hat.

Trudi opened the conversation about what the magazine needed technology-wise. She suggested that he phone her the next day about making an appointment to come in sometime in the next week to assess their requirements. Michael was happy. The conversation had been to the point and the matter sorted in a clean ten minutes. He could soon finish off his brandy and get back to London. In fact he was already feeling slightly intoxicated from the copious amounts of alcohol his hosts were supplying him with. Trudi topped up his brandy glass, again.

Rupert motioned as if he were about to say something so Michael waited, but nothing came, only more silence. Rupert had taken the riding crop in his left hand and was gently stroking the underneath of his wife's chin with the leather thong at the end.

"Michael, do you think my wife is attractive?"

There was a silence as Michael pondered as to whether he had heard incorrectly. If there was going to be games, he was quite happy to play.

"Yeah. She's an attractive woman," he said calmly and straight.

"Would you like to fuck her, Michael?"

"No Rupert, what you want to ask is, 'Michael will you fuck my wife for me while I watch'?"

Rupert smiled deviously and moved the end of the riding crop to Trudi's right nipple and started to make slow circular motions on her jumper.

"Do you like her breasts, Michael?"

Trudi sat lounging back in the sofa expressionless, but studying Michael's reaction closely.

Rupert squeezed his wife's breast firmly in his hand.

"My wife tells me you are quite an accomplished fucker."

Michael shifted uneasily in his seat. He wasn't sure what was going down here, and he didn't know if it meant trouble. Rupert could read his thoughts.

"Oh don't worry, Trudi has told me all about Heathrow. Everything is fine. You can relax. You see Michael, I find it very satisfying when another man sleeps with my wife. It's an immense turn-on. It's an even bigger turn-on when I can watch my wife being taken." Rupert smiled. "Trudi tells me you're hung like a horse."

Now Michael understood the game plan and he didn't have any problems with it. It wasn't the first time he'd been in this scenario. He had seen the 'inadequate white man asking black stud to fuck the missus' before. If that was what sad old Rupert wanted, then he would get it. He would enjoy humiliating the millionaire and giving that bitch a boning she wouldn't forget in a hurry.

Michael got to his feet and told the woman to take off her clothes. She eagerly obliged and was soon standing naked on the rug in front of the fire, the flames creating a glow on her white skin.

Michael had also stripped naked and had lowered Trudi to her knees. He stood above her, his large hands gripping the back of her head. She held the back of his thighs tightly, pressing her fingers into his flesh. Slowly, he pulled her face towards his groin and she hungrily started to lick, suck and kiss his penis and testicles in an almost desperate manner.

"Gosh, you weren't exaggerating old girl, were you? He's hung like a donkey!" exclaimed Rupert.

Once she had sufficiently feasted to raise him into action, Michael positioned Trudi over a small footstool with her bottom raised up in the air. She meekly awaited her punishment, her eyes darting around in anticipation. Michael picked up the riding crop from the table and raised his hand up. With a swift stroke, he brought the leather thong down onto her bare buttocks with a loud 'thwack'.

Trudi inhaled a loud breath and awaited further discipline. Again, he brought the crop down on her buttocks. Then again, and again. Strawberry coloured welts slowly started to rise on the white flesh of her bottom. She was moaning in ecstasy. Laying down the crop, Michael slipped his hand between her tights and felt the wetness of her pussy. Her moistness was seeping forth into her brown pubic hairs, which glistened in the fire's glow. He knelt down on the rug and used his right hand to guide his swollen cock into the entrance of her vagina. With a slow forwards movement of his pelvis, he thrust his dark cock into the soft pinkness of her pussy. He pushed it right up to the hilt and she let out an agonising moan of pleasure. He moved more and more vigorously, giving her pussy all the 'agony' it could take.

The wife moaned and screamed begging for it to be given to her 'harder'. She sounded not like someone in pain, but like someone enjoying the ride of their life.

Michael continued to ram her pussy with all his energy, clenching his buttocks for extra force. He pumped rhythmically, watching the muscles in her back flex up and down, his large ebony hands gripping her pelvis. Then he stopped abruptly. The room was silent. She continued to pant, wondering what was happening. He wanted her to know who was in control. He pulled out slowly, until his head met the lips of her vagina. For a moment all was still, even Rupert stopped his fumblings. He then shot his dick forward, so quickly and deep, she screamed in shock. He did it again, then again; his timing was impeccable. She thrashed her head like a wild animal, in appreciation of his skill.

It was time to try a new position. He moved the stool away and rolled Trudi onto her back. The tried and trusted missionary position would do just fine. Pushing her down on the rug, he supported his body with his hands and raised himself off her chest. He wanted to savour the sight of his erect manhood moving in and out of her vagina.

From the sofa, DeBorchgrave urged the jockey to ride her with vigour.

"Harder Michael. Fuck her, fuck her!!"

The salesman didn't need to be told. He was already steadily working his tool away, filling her pussy with his firm erect flesh. Her moans were rapid and deep in tone. Each gasp of pleasure reverberating around the room. Rupert was chanting under his breath. "Yes, yes, yes, yes!"

As she got nearer to climax, Michael pushed her legs together and pulled himself further up her body, so that the shaft of his penis rubbed firmly on her clitoris. Within moments, Trudi was screaming with ecstasy as the soaring climax gripped her, sending her body into convulsions of joy. Michael was nearly there. As he reached the point of no return, he withdrew to kneel over and send a stream of hot semen over her breasts and face. He shook the last drops of semen over her mouth with his hand and looked down at her while her fingers maintained the climax.

Michael strode coolly across the room to his pile of clothes laying carefully across the armchair. As he searched for his boxer shorts, he noticed DeBorchgrave adjusting his flies.

"Bloody good show, Michael. I've watched many men fuck my wife, but I've never seen stamina like that before."

"My pleasure Rupert, anytime you want her serviced let me know." His comment was laced with sarcasm.

Strange, fucked-up power games thought Michael. There really wasn't anything as strange, sexually, as the English upper classes. Maybe it was because they had the money to indulge their fantasies and fetishes. Or maybe it was their sheer arrogance and self-confidence that allowed them to explore every area of their sexuality without any sense of guilt, self-consciousness or doubt.

Trudi reminded him of Jemima, that Sloanie girl who ran her own PR company in Chelsea. The living Sloanie fe true. That girl had more kinks than a rubber hose and didn't give a damn. If she wanted to do it; she'd do it. Jemima had this strong, exhibitionist streak in her sexual make-up. She enjoyed leaving the light on and the curtains open when she got undressed at night so that her neighbour's 16-year-old son could watch her undress and masturbate from his bedroom window.

Not only that, Jemima would go out wearing the shortest of skirts and no underwear. On buses and the tube, she would open her legs so that the male passengers would gain a discreet view of her. She said it used to turn her on seeing the bulging erections in men's trousers when she gave her private viewings.

Such was her love of public exposure that she and Michael once had sex in Gloucester Road tube station. It may not have been rush hour, but the platform was still busy. She stood against a wall with one leg curled around his torso and he took her slowly, with her arms hugging him as if in an innocent embrace, while concealing his actions with his long coat. Now there was an experience to remember!

After dressing and leaving the room, Trudi returned with a tray of coffee and biscuits. The group sat around engaging in polite conversation and acting as though nothing out of the ordinary had just taken place. The only clues lay in the stained carpet and Trudi's smile.

Rupert telephoned his chauffeur who lived a few miles away and summoned him to the house to drive his guest back to London. Once again, Michael contemplated the power of money. Although it was nearly 11.00pm, Rupert was obviously paying the driver well enough that he could summon him at whatever time he required him.

Within twenty minutes the driver had arrived. Michael thanked the DeBorchgrave's for their hospitality and bizarre entertainment and reminded Trudi that he would call her the next day about the computers. Then he climbed into the Mercedes and headed back to London.

On the journey along the M25 Michael sprawled out in the sumptuous leather back seat of 500SE Merc. This was the life he wanted. Coincidences really did happen. The day that he nearly decided to give a miss had produced some excellent returns. All he had to do was exploit this special relationship he had established with the DeBorchgraves. If it meant giving his wife some action, it didn't matter. He was always giving with women, but he rarely ever gained financially from it. No, this was a golden opportunity. He just had to make sure he used it to the max.

ELEVEN

"I'm sorry Michael, but I don't buy that. At some point, black men have got to take personal responsibility for their actions."

Monica Bramble left her comment floating in the air and lifted her wine glass to her mouth. The conversation had moved into Michael's danger territory, which was not to his liking. The discussion had somehow got on to the subject of baby fathers. Michael had tried to defend the problem of absentee fathers by portioning blame on racism and the breakdown of the family structure through slavery. But Monica was having none of it.

"I admit black men do need to do a serious amount of prioritising to get their house in order. I accept that."

He hoped that would end the conversation and then they could just enjoy the ambience of the restaurant.

"You're probably right too, history does have something to do with it, but if we are going to move on, we have to overcome those elements and deal with what we do as individuals on a day to day basis." He knew this line of discussion was not going to rest. After all, he thought, he was laying out "nuff dollars' for the meal.

Roberto's — which overlooked the river near Chelsea Harbour — was reputed to be one of the finest Italian restaurants in London and was a popular soirée point for media celebrities and their agents. Tastefully decorated in classical Neapolitan style, circular tables were covered with hand-embroidered, linen table clothes and each table was illuminated with a discreet silver candelabra. In summer, the conservatory doors at the end of the restaurant would open to let the cool breeze from the river waft through to the diners.

In the corner, a pianist at a grand piano was playing a relaxing blend of classic jazz bar tunes while the other diners savoured their exquisite dishes.

Michael had earlier picked Monica up from her office and whisked her off to the restaurant without telling her their destination for the evening. She was impressed with his choice of eatery and he was glad that he'd gone to the expense of the evening. Things had gone well and they quickly started to feel relaxed in each other's company.

"I have to say, before our conversation takes us further, you look stunning tonight. It's not many women who can come from a day at work and still completely fit in with these sophisticated surroundings."

"Thanking you kindly, Mr. Hughes. A dynamic woman such as myself has to accessorise you know." Her over the top English accent was put to great effect. "It's amazing what one can do with a string of pearls and two hair clips."

They both broke into a satisfying laugh.

She wore a classic, black double-breasted trouser suit, with a cream camisole making a small appearance from underneath and two pins were used, to sweep up her hair into a perfect French roll. Her outfit was completed by a broad choker of pearls, which emphasised her slender neck.

For his part, Michael was very impressed with his dinner date. It was not that often that he met a woman who so encapsulated all the things a man could want. She looked incredibly beautiful and she was amusing, intelligent and ambitious but relaxed about it. He had previously found it hard to gel with ambitious sisters who thought they were in competition with black men, but Monica displayed her desire to excel with honesty. If you know you have it, why do you need to prove it to others, he reasoned? She was obviously of the same opinion.

Monica was definitely the sort of woman he could hang with, without the 'Wanderer Factor'. He recalled a friend saying that the reason some black men had various women was because they sought perfection. But as there was no such thing as the perfect woman they found pieces of perfection in different women. There would be one who could cook well, another who was a great conversationalist, another who was sexual heaven, and so on and so forth. This refusal to 'compromise' was what led to multiple relationships: 'the Wanderer Factor'.

Monica finished her glass of wine and looked to Michael.

"I don't mean to get heavy about things over dinner, but I do feel there needs to be some major changes in black male attitudes."

Monica was testing Michael's resilience with every word. She ensured the conversation would not shift away from this topic, to make him indeed work hard. He decided to pretend his mouth was full of food to avoid saying anything more.

"It's not about sex. I think if two people decide that they're gonna have a casual sexual relationship, that's fine. But if a child comes from that union, then the man has got to deal with his responsibility. You've got a situation now with a lot of single women who are dependent on the state for their existence and it's destroying our independence as a community."

Michael had to act quickly if he was to sustain any type of parity during this date. He decided a change was in order.

"How's the computer going?"

Monica took the hint.

"Okay, fine. It's nice to finally have something that's up to the job."

Before he could add anything, his mobile interrupted. He'd forgotten to switch it off. Monica's expression said it all, she was obviously not impressed. Michael sheepishly flipped open his phone.

"Hello."

"Michael it's Shantelle here. I really need to speak to you now."

"It's a bit inconvenient right now. Let me phone you back later."

"No, Michael I need to speak to you right now."

"Look I'm in the middle of doing something. I'll call you later."

"Please Michael. I'm asking you, please speak to me now."

This verbal ping-pong was getting him nowhere. To prevent Shantelle from completely destroying his evening, he had to think quickly.

"Right okay, that's good news."

"You're with another woman? Who is the bitch? Don't fucking lie to me Michael."

"Yeah. Excellent."

"You fucking shit. I'll fucking…"

"Good one. Speak to you later, bye." With that he pressed the 'off' button.

The call had taken him by surprise and he was feeling flustered. It showed.

Monica smiled and shook her head.

"You men. You always dig holes for yourselves. I know she was annoyed, but if a women is going to call me a bitch, I like to have done something to her first."

Michael tried to hide his embarrassment. He made a mental note to get rid of this mobile in the morning, it was too bloody loud for his liking.

"Oh no, it was nothing like that. Just a business colleague."

Monica didn't believe it and she was going to let him know it.

"What is it with guys, why do they find it so difficult to tell another woman that they are sleeping with someone else? You're clearly not the Virgin Mary. I mean, how many men sleep with just one woman?"

Michael realised he'd been rumbled and it would be worse to continue the lie.

"Okay, I'm sorry I lied. It's just someone I occasionally see. It's nothing serious, just a casual t'ing."

"So why lie Michael, do you think it'll effect your chances of getting me into bed?"

He was taken aback by her directness.

"Bwoy you're certainly direct and to the point aren't you, Monica?"

"Oh come off it Michael, it's something we're both thinking about. You've not taken me out to an expensive restaurant just because you want to be my friend. This is an investment, and you want your payback. Like most guys you're testing the water to see if anything's gonna bite. True?"

He was being put on the spot so decided he'd be as direct as she was.

"Okay. The thought has crossed my mind." He added. "I could think of more unpleasant things than spending a night in bed with you. And while we're being blunt and to the point, what are you scouting for?"

Monica played it cool to the end.

"I don't know you, Michael. I always check out all the angles before I commit myself to any course of action."

He thought now was an appropriate moment to declare 'time out' in the mind games; he made his excuses and headed to the bathroom.

As he washed his hands, Michael looked at his features in the mirror above the wash basin and heaved a deep sigh.

"This woman is putting me through some hoops, but I'm harder than the best. The Mighty Michael is in full effect. I can't afford to blow this one 'cause Monica is fly. Some serious tactics are needed here. But bwoy, you're getting too old for all this ducking and diving shit, you'll get a heart attack." He warned his reflection.

It was a strange evening, sometimes the mood was light and relaxing and at other times it lapsed into mental duelling. It certainly kept him on his toes, as he never quite knew where the mood was going to swing.

This woman wasn't going to be easy to bullshit. She'd already caught him out once tonight and he certainly didn't want to be shown up again. The tactic was set: he would proceed with a degree of caution and make sure that his tracks were very carefully covered.

They ordered coffees and sat talking about their life histories and family backgrounds. Monica was six months older than Michael and like Michael she was born and bred in London. However, she was 'only a West London gyal', he teased, having grown up in Ealing.

She had grown up in a comfortable middle class home — her father being a businessman — and when she and her two sisters were older, her mother trained as an accountant and established her own accountancy practice in Chiswick.

Of her two younger sisters, one was an accountant working in her mother's business and the other worked for the Department of Transport as a statistician.

"I think it must be in the genes," Monica explained. "Everyone in the family is mathematically minded. My father used to sit us down when we were kids and teach us about profit and loss accounts and percentages. My mother told him that seven was a bit young for that kind of teaching, but I'm sure it set us on the right track."

Monica was obviously close to her father, but her tone was full of regret. She explained that when they were children, their father had been too busy with his property development business to give them as much attention as they would have liked.

"I think my mother was a bit hard on the old man when we were younger. She was a very demanding woman and I think it was only when she had her own career that she realised how much time a business takes."

"Yeah tell me about it," Michael sympathised. "Sorry to cut you Monica, don't stop."

"No, I think I've revealed enough about myself for one night. A girl has to have some mystique, you know. Let's get down to the nitty gritty. What was your first sexual experience?"

Monica wasn't messing about, but Michael was prepared to match her punch for punch. He took a sip of his Perrier, and pondered his answer.

"I suppose it would have to be when I was fourteen. I had a brief t'ing with a friend of mine's mother. Joan was in her mid-forties with four children and lived near us in Brockley. I was good friends with her son, Devon, who was in my class at school.

It was the summer holidays and I went round to see if Devon was in, one Saturday afternoon. Most times he was in the garden fixing up his bike, so I thought I'd sneak up the path at the side of the house and jump out on him. Well, I went round the back of the house, but Devon wasn't there. The doors to their through lounge were open and the TV was on. It made sense to figure that he was watching TV, wouldn't you say?" Monica nodded, engrossed in the build up in Michael's tale. "So I went through the door and stumbled upon his mum sitting on the sofa, her skirt pulled up and working herself off with a vibrator. I was so shocked I froze on the spot."

"What did you do?" Monica eagerly enquired.

"Let me tell the story nuh. Anyway, she called me over to her like she was well vexed, but her mood soon changed as she made me use the vibrator on her. So I'm fumbling around with this thing, still in a state of shock until she shows me exactly what to do. Once I'd mastered it, I started to get turned on, and she noticed it. Well she mek me tek off me trousers and she starts feel up my t'ings!" Monica chuckled at his Caribbean accent. "I was really excited, but scared in case someone caught us. It turned out that everyone was out for the day. But anyway, this woman started to suck me and it felt wicked. By this point, I'd almost fainted, but she carried on doing t'ings with various parts of her body on different parts of my body that I feel would be totally unsuitable for dinner conversation."

Monica looked like she had been robbed of the winning National Lottery ticket by Michael's sudden display of chivalry.

As a consolation, he elaborated slightly.

"Well, put it this way, she is the one that taught me that sex is more than just intercourse. I went round there a few times during the summer, but we never actually had sex. The funny thing about it is that years later, my mother made some joke remark about how I used to like Joan when I was a boy. To this day, I wonder if she suspects something went down with Joan. But how could she? I can't think that there was anything to give her any clues and I never used to tell her where I was going. That's parent's for you. Always reading your mind."

Michael slumped back in his chair, satisfied that he had told an entertaining story in the true Alex style.

"So come on Monica, the tables have to turn now. Your

go."

"Excuse me?"

"Ah, come on Monica, there's me, pouring my sexual heart out to you. I deserve a little something from you, don't I?" Michael sounded almost desperate in his plea.

"Okay, okay, keep your shirt on, what do you want to know?"

"What was your first sexual experience?"

"Michael, I can't tell you that. It's very private — more than a grope with your mate's mum. I haven't known you long enough to tell you those kind of details about myself."

Monica cut the conversation dead. She obviously made that statement from the heart, and Michael almost felt guilty for asking.

"Okay, 'nuff said."

"What I *will* tell you is my best sexual experience." A broad smile crossed Monica's face as she sprang up in her seat.

"Well, when I was working for an American music magazine, I was flown to the Bahamas for a music conference. Anyway, I had seen this guy on the plane over who was drop dead gorgeous." Michael wriggled in his seat.

"We never spoke but we often looked at each other across the aisle. So, I was in my hotel room relaxing, when there's a knock at the door. I opened it to find Mr. Tall, Dark and Handsome there with a crushed shirt in his hand. He asked me if he could borrow an iron. I couldn't believe my luck, he was in the room next door to me. I lent him mine, of course, it was the only thing to do. Anyway, on returning the iron he offered to take me out to dinner as a thank-you. I accepted and we enjoyed a sumptuous seafood gumbo at the Beach restaurant."

Michael almost choked on his drink. Could Barbara be haunting him?

"Are you alright, Michael? Yeah? Okay, I'll finish the story. After getting slightly tipsy with the Rum cocktails, we decided to rent a boat to go to one of the smaller islands. As

114

soon as we got onto the boat we started kissing and touching each other in all the right places. At this stage, a storm started to brew, and the boat began to rock violently. We were both so absorbed physically, we just let the boat float out to sea. The storm sent hot rain down onto our bodies as we had sex on the deck for hours. I can feel that rain now. I've never felt anything like it. It must have been a good few hours before we woke and realised that we were fifteen miles out to sea. We called the coastguard, who came to rescue us. We entertained ourselves, of course, until they arrived."

"What happened to the guy?" Michael enquired, wishing he'd had such a story to tell.

"We spent a lot of time together on the trip, but he lived in New York, whilst I was living in Atlanta. You could call him the one who got away." Monica's voice was slightly lamentful as she bit into the final after dinner mint.

"Bwoy, you won't catch me and my 'cyaan swim' black ass sexing anyone in a boat miles out to sea."

They both laughed to the point of crying.

With the mood so jovial, Michael suggested that he sort out the bill and they head to a casino to watch the action and have a drink.

A photographer friend had introduced him to many of London's casinos. If you knew someone who was already a member it wasn't difficult to gain membership yourself. Casinos, the friend told him, were good places to take clients or women because the atmosphere was glamourous and the food and drink were not expensive, to encourage the gamblers into the establishments.

Outside The Riviera, just off exclusive Park Lane, Michael pulled the BMW up behind a Jaguar. The casino attracted a cosmopolitan range of patrons and a group of wealthy African businessmen were just walking up the stairs to the imposing entrance, as Michael opened the car door for Monica. He handed the keys to a valet who was parking the customers' cars.

Housed in a stylish, columned neo-classical building,

The Riviera had an impressive but discreet, varnished wooden door. Lit by two polished brass lamps on the wall, the building's facade contained no visual information that the venue was a casino. A small brass sign inscribed with the street number and the name were the only markings. A doorman in top hat and white gloves waited outside to open the door for guests.

Walking through to a reception area, Michael produced his membership card to a young woman and signed the membership book. A red-carpeted foyer led into the main part of the casino where three roulette tables were interspersed with blackjack tables. The mix of ethnic groups was intriguing. At the table nearest to the entrance sat the Chinese whose serious faces studied the roulette wheel carefully. On other tables sat Arabs, Africans and Europeans.

It was the first time Monica had been to a casino and she was quite excited by the atmosphere. Wearing her business suit, she felt not quite appropriately dressed among the black gowned women, but she still made heads turn. It was the atmosphere she had seen in countless films, but never imagined she would be part of.

"So Michael, how long have you been an international playboy?" she whispered in his ear, her eyes soaking up all the activity around her.

"Well, really an' truly you know baby, I man, is more an international yardie. You understan'? London, Paris, Kingston. When my yacht nah off French Riviera, me just haffe double park it in Mo' Bay. Yuh understan'?"

A waiter passing with a bottle of champagne did a double take at Michael and Monica as they fell about laughing.

"Listen Mikey Dread, me nah t'ink dem is ready for yardie yet, star," joked Monica about the casino's staff.

It was the first time Michael had heard her speak in anything other than her 'correct' English accent.

"So Monica, yuh turn yardie now?"

"Listen Michael darling," she mocked in her best toffee

116

nosed accent, "I'll have you know that some of my best friends are coloured," she grinned, nodding her head. "Fe true, Michael."

Michael laughed and squeezed her waist. He moved to kiss her neck, but she pushed him away playfully.

"Unh-unh! Don't jump the gun."

She was deadly serious, but managed nevertheless to make her point with humour.

They walked through the main roulette area and took a seat in the plush Le Jardin bar. Creatively styled with exotic plants and a small fountain, the bar really did have a French garden feel to it. A waiter quickly approached and took their order. He returned shortly after with two brandies. Raising his glass, Michael proposed a toast.

"To the good times, may they keep on rolling."

"To the good times," Monica agreed, knocking her glass with his.

"Well, this has been a fun evening, Mr Hughes. Thank you for showing me a good time."

"I've enjoyed myself, too. Listen Monica, I don't know if you have any plans for Sunday. My brother is having a lunch party and wants me to bring a respectable woman along. Well, I immediately thought of you."

"What makes you think I'm respectable?" she purred.

"I didn't say you were respectable. I just said 'I immediately thought of you'."

"Feisty man," she cried in pretend outrage. "Michael, you're lucky because for once, this Sunday is free. But in future, don't jus' t'ink you can fling down appointment like so, at short notice. Yuh understan'?"

"So Monica, we have a future? That's nice to know," he said sarcastically.

She kissed her teeth and finished her drink. Then they made their way over to the cashier where he bought £100 in roulette chips.

"Okay baby, you better bring me some luck", he told her. He offered his arm and they strolled elegantly to a couple of empty seats at the nearest table.

The Jewish-looking man next to them smiled and said 'hello' as Monica took her seat at the green, felt-topped table. An assorted group of people sat around the table. To the croupier's right, sat a Middle Eastern playboy type followed by an elderly white couple. Next to them, was a smooth-looking Italian. A real diverse bunch of people brought together by the love of the gambling.

"Place your bets, please," said the croupier.

Various denominations of chips were placed onto the table by the players. Monica outstretched her hand.

"The lady is in control tonight," she declared, as Michael graciously handed over the chips. She placed three £5 blue chips on the broad twelve number block of 'black 10's'.

"No more bets, please." Instructed the croupier as he studied the table carefully. He sent the small, white ball on its way as he spun the wheel in the opposing direction. The ball spun furiously around the inside of the wheel, rattling along until it bounced into fate's designated spot.

"Black 17", called the croupier.

Monica gave Michael a reassuring grin, as her winnings were pushed back to her position.

"It looks like lady luck is called Monica tonight," he joked.

"Some may call it luck, others would call it skill. 'Red 40' is what this lady feels."

"Do what you gotta do, but if you lose all my money, you owe me," Michael whispered into her ear.

Monica slipped the chips over to the intersection which included her lucky number with confidence.

"We'll see".

When the ball landed on 'Red 38', Michael almost screamed with delight. Once again, the croupier slid their winnings over.

"Do you trust me, Michael?" Monica had a mischievous look as she spoke.

"Yes." Michael couldn't believe he had just said that. Before he could take the all-important word back, Monica had moved the entire pile of chips, worth about £400, onto one area.

"All on black 11," she declared.

"All of it?" Michael exclaimed. "You serious, all our chips?"

"What's the matter, Michael, you said you trusted me."

"Yeah, but four hundred smackers is a lot of trust. How about half?" Michael had a pleading expression, which drew Monica's sympathy, but at a price.

"Okay, but if I win, I get to keep all the winnings."

Michael contemplated the deal. If she lost all the money, he would have nothing, but if she won he would still have around double his initial investment. Not great odds, but not bad. Although Michael had not realised, the entire table, as well as Monica, were awaiting his response. No one dared breath and the elderly woman looked like she was about to pass out with anticipation. Even the croupier was gripped.

"Last bets, please."

Michael stroked his beard. The Jewish man couldn't take anymore.

"Come on, let the woman have her winnings."

"Alright Monica, you can have the winnings."

She smiled as she piled roughly half the chips onto 'Black 11'. The table's other occupants feverishly slipped chips onto 'Black 11', ranging from £100 from the 'playboy' to £20 from the elderly couple. The old man would have put more, but was restrained by his wife, as she noticed him give Monica a quick wink.

The Jewish man smiled with reassurance.

"In this game, it's always best to go on your gut feeling. If you don't win, then you can only lose." He stacked £150 onto the crowded number.

"No more bets."

The wheel spun furiously with the ball whirling round the chromed rim. As it slowed, Michael could hardly look. The table groaned as the ball rolled into 'Red 18' then their yelps could be heard from as far as the bar, as it jumped out into 'Black 13'.

Michael looked at Monica in disbelief. Even the Casino Supervisor made an appearance as the croupier doubled everyone's stake. Monica exchanged her multitude of chips for four golden discs, along with a couple of smaller denominations. Michael was still slightly in awe at what he had just witnessed.

"Michael, does the word 'gutted' come to mind?"

He could only concede monetary defeat, as they made their way to the Cashier's desk. Monica was loving every minute of it, but didn't want Michael to feel too dejected.

"Well, we certainly have a future now. You have to help me spend this money." She joked.

The valet drove the BMW to the front of The Riviera and the couple headed south to Monica's place in South Wimbledon. She'd said she could take a cab home as she could now afford it, but Michael insisted he drop her off.

On the drive over Westminster Bridge they were both silent, only Anita Baker's sultry tones filled the car with sound. Monica was sleepy, her head turned towards the window, clutching her winnings in a velvet drawstring purse provided by the casino. Michael had not felt so relaxed in the company of a woman for a long time. They didn't feel the need to talk about anything, they simply existed, and he found this state of affairs refreshingly attractive.

"Please, God. Don't let me fuck this up."

Monica smiled and closed her eyes.

Michael was so at ease that by the time they reached South Wimbledon tube station it seemed that only ten minutes had passed since they left the casino. He gently touched Monica's shoulder to wake her.

"Monica, we're in South Wimbledon. Where do you live?" His soft tone roused her out of her slumber and she directed him into a quiet road of neat 1930's semi-detached houses. Her home was number 184, right at the end.

She was now wide awake as they pulled up outside. Michael took off his seat belt and turned to face her. She got in first.

"Well, Michael, what a night. Thanks again."

Michael licked his lips discreetly. She kissed him on the cheek.

"What, don't I even get coffee?"

Walking to her front door, she smiled and blew him a kiss.

"I never serve coffee on a first date. See you on Sunday."

As Michael pulled away, he noticed an upstairs light was on. *She reached upstairs quickly,* he thought.

TWELVE

Marcus was in a restless mood and determined that his little sister Bianca would not be allowed to play peacefully on her own. He grabbed one of the Barbie dolls she was playing with and held it in front of her face, teasing. When she attempted to retrieve it, he would pull it away from reach of her grip.

"Give me my Barbie back Marcus."

The demand simply encouraged the small boy further in his annoyance. He held the doll's body in one hand, and the head in the other. He acted as if attempting to pull off the head, which only stirred up his sister more. With a shriek, she made a frantic grab for her prized Barbie, knocking Marcus against the ceramic plant pot stand near the glass topped coffee table. The pedestal toppled, sending the plant pot crashing down on the table's glass top. Marcus froze in fear.

"What the hell are you children doing?" came his mother's angry shout from the kitchen.

By the time Diane Hughes had stormed into the front room, Marcus' bottom lip was trembling and he was pointing an accusing finger at his sister.

"Mummy, it was her fault. It was her fault."

Bianca was getting hysterical and tears started to pour.

"He was going to pull Barbie's head off. Ahhhhhhhh."

Miraculously, neither the plant pot or the coffee table top were damaged.

"Marcus, go to the kitchen and get the dust pan and brush."

With head bowed, the youngster did as he was told.

In the meantime, Diane did her best to calm her daughter.

"Don't worry Bianca, stop crying. Barbie is alright. Just ignore Marcus when he's being foolish or just come and tell me."

She picked up the plant stand and positioned it back in its original place with the leafy plant on top.

Marcus walked sheepishly back in the front room with his cleaning instruments.

"Right. I want every spec of soil off this carpet and if I hear another word out of you this afternoon, boy you're in trouble. You hear me?" She warned the eight year old.

Ten minutes later, the upstairs bathroom door opened and Josey stuck his head out.

"What's going on down there?"

He came down the stairs in a bathrobe and looked suspiciously at Marcus.

"Marcus, I hope you're not troubling your sister again because you know I'll have to trouble you if you are."

Diane and Josey had got up early this Sunday to prepare the food for their guests coming round for lunch. They'd invited Diane's brother Trevor and his wife Veronica, plus Michael and unknown partner. They were making sure everything would be just right for their lunch guests and the last thing an already stressed Diane needed was Marcus' antics.

Seeing that normality had been re-established, Josey went back upstairs and quickly got dressed. He returned to the front room to check that Marcus was behaving himself, then went to help his wife in the kitchen.

Josey and Diane's South Woodford 1960's built semi was typical of the many comfortable middle class family homes in the area. With a neat front garden and garage it was the sort of house where, on a Sunday, husbands would be cleaning the company car while the wife prepared lunch. It was a quiet neighbourhood where a couple could raise their kids away from the hustle and bustle of the inner city. They were grateful that they could afford to raise Marcus and Bianca in a peaceful area and send them to good schools. It meant both of them having to work and make certain sacrifices to give their kids the best possible start in life, but it was worth it .

They'd lived there since Marcus was born eight years ago and Diane had given up her job at the local education authority. She took five years away from work to look after her family and when she went back to the education department, she worked a job share which gave her more flexibility with the children and their school.

Diane was happy. She was married to a man she loved, had two lovely children and a nice home. At times she wished Josey didn't have to work so hard, but she knew he was doing it for her and the kids. Still she worried he would burn himself out.

For Josey, hard work was a necessity of life. 'Nothing comes easy' was his motto and he reasoned that with the world being what it was, it was even more difficult for the black man. Although on the surface he didn't appear to be a very political person, Josey had deep seated concerns about where the black community was heading. He was a strong believer in the principals of family life and was worried about the growing lack of involvement of black men in raising their children. It was a sore topic of conversation between him and his brother. They had very different perspectives on life and both had agreed to disagree a long time ago.

Back in the kitchen, Diane was checking that the chicken in the oven was roasting well. Josey was busy cutting up some carrots on the chopping board next to the sink. It was still some while before their guests would arrive, but the couple wanted to get everything prepared in time so Josey could have a moment to sit and play with the children. The weekend was the only time he really saw them. By the time he got in from work in the evenings they were already in bed, and in the mornings he was on his way to Mac In-Touch before they were up and about.

With the immediate kitchen chores done Diane and Josey joined the kids in the front room. Marcus lay on the carpet reading a book and Bianca was busy beautifying her black Barbie doll. Marcus was initially a reluctant book reader, but in the last year he had really taken a liking to it. Diane had put strict controls on the time he spent watching TV and playing with his computer games, leaving him with little choice but to pick up a book. He had now caught the reading bug and had become an inspired pupil, as his class teacher was quick to point out.

The mutual consensus was for everyone to play Ludo so Marcus went to retrieve the board game from his bedroom.

Diane set up the game and after some haggling between Marcus and Bianca as to who was going to be red, she was able to persuade her daughter that blue was just as nice a colour.

Blue proved to be today's lucky colour. Every other roll of the dice seemed to be coming up 'six' for Bianca and she was taking a commanding lead over the other players. Marcus was not pleased at his older sister's lucky streak and got irritated with her squeal of delight and clapping when a 'six' came up again. His father had to warn him about poor sportsmanship when he tried to surreptitiously move one of Bianca's counters back to the starting base. Poor Marcus, it just wasn't his day.

With a huge measure of luck and some well thought out tactical play, Bianca took the board by storm. In what seemed like the shortest Ludo game in the Hughes' family history, Bianca finally brought the last of her counters home. A loud round of self-congratulations followed the hand clapping. Bianca destroyed Marcus' will to compete. Sulkily, he said he didn't want to play anymore and resumed his prior position on the lounge carpet. No amount of coaxing could change his position on the matter, so Diane returned to the kitchen, while Josey helped choose a suitable outfit for Barbie's night out at the disco.

Trevor and Veronica were the first to arrive and seemed in happy spirits. Three years older than Diane, Trevor had always been very much 'big brother' to her. From childhood days he had always been there looking out for 'little sis' and theirs had been a close relationship. A short stocky man, friends joked that he looked like Richard Pryor, due to his moustache and mini afro. Veronica, a small slender woman, was seven years Trevor's junior but looked even younger than that. They had been married two years and both still worked for the same City insurance firm where they had met only a year before their wedding.

Diane showed them into the lounge, while Josey opened a bottle of wine in the kitchen.

"Haven't those two grown," Veronica remarked about Bianca and Marcus.

"Yeah. I'm preparing myself for when they want to borrow my car," quipped Josey, handing the guests wine glasses.

"The question is when am I gonna get the chance to comment on how quickly your pickney are growing? I need a fellow daddy to empathise with down the pub on a Sunday lunch time." He'd teased Trevor many times before on the subject and he couldn't resist the opportunity now.

Trevor looked at Veronica with a wide grin on his face.

"Should I?"

Veronica smiled and nodded.

"Well papa Josey, I'll have a pint of lager. I am proud to announce that in eight months there is going to be a new resident at the Simms' household."

Josey let out a cowboy yelp and offered his hand to his brother-in-law.

"Congratulations. Big up yuhself, Mr Simms. Me nevah t'ink you had it in you." He added. "Fling away that wine. We should be drinking champers."

With that, Josey disappeared to the kitchen and returned with a bottle of champagne they had left over from Christmas.

Diane hugged her brother and his wife then started the interrogation that was usual of an expectant mother. When did she find out? Did she want a boy or girl? Had they thought about names?

They had only found out in the last week and not really had time to think about all these things, explained Veronica. Having only decided a few months ago to start a family, the couple were overjoyed with the news.

The adults' excitement had aroused Bianca's curiosity and she was pulling her mother's skirt to get her attention.

"Mummy, Mummy what's happened?"

"Auntie Veronica is going to have a baby. So you will have a cousin to play with."

Bianca contemplated the prospect for a moment then with a look of concern, asked a pertinent question.

"If it's a girl will she want to play with my Barbie?"

Poor Bianca couldn't understand why the grown ups should find her query in the least bit amusing, so she looked puzzled when the room broke into laughter.

The ring of the doorbell brought a pause to the merriment. Josey went to open the front door.

"So who's won the lottery? I could hear the excitement from down the street."

Michael had arrived with Monica. After introducing her, they wandered into the lounge where Michael again introduced his friend.

"You've both arrived at exactly the right time. Trevor has just announced that he's going to be a father."

"Do we know the woman?" It was one of Michael's usual bad taste jokes but Veronica knew him and wasn't offended.

Trevor was quick with a response. Pointing to Michael he asked: "Does anyone know him?"

"Joke me ah joke, iyah. No seriously, congratulations. And it's not before time. But you know I was always sticking up for you Trev, I used to say, 'nah, the man ain't that way inclined'. Now I don't have to."

Trevor pointed again. "No seriously, does anyone know how this man got past security?"

Michael and Trevor did a spot of playful sparring then shook hands warmly.

"Well Michael, it looks like it's your turn to do something for world under population," teased Trevor," as they say, the balls are in your court."

"My balls can definitely stay caught right where they belong, thank you. No star, dis farmer nuh ready fe sowing any seed right now." As he made the jest, he suddenly remembered Jackie and wondered if his words would come back to haunt him.

Everyone was curious as to who this attractive woman

with Michael was and it wasn't long before Diane had offered Monica a drink and begun quizzing her.

"Ladies and gentlemen, oh and Michael," joked Josey, "luncheon is about to be served in the dinning room. If you would like to follow me , I will show you to your seats."

The group squeezed round the dinning table at the other end of the lounge and Josey and Diane started to bring the various dishes to the table. It was traditional Sunday fare of chicken, rice and peas, vegetables, plantain and some sweet potatoes. It looked and smelt delicious.

Bianca had taken a liking to Monica and was sitting next to her at the table watching her closely.

"You look like my Barbie," Bianca told her sweetly.

Monica smiled.

"Ahh," she cooed. "Now why couldn't a man say something as sweet as that?"

"I don't know too many men who've got their own Barbie doll. Maybe that's why," Michael joked, adding, "but then again Trev didn't you once tell me…"

He'd caught Trevor with a mouthful of food so he could only fight back with a loud mumble and by pointing a fork at his tormentor.

"Ah, poor Trevor, he doesn't deserve it," Diane pleaded.

Michael moved closer to Monica and pointed to Trevor. "Don't listen to Di. He may look totally harmless, but that man is vicious. If you don't get a few blows in first, he'll knock you down in the first round. Believe me."

"Yeah," Veronica agreed, "he gives as good as he gets. But I think Michael might just be ahead on points."

Trevor disagreed.

"It's early yet. I've still got the old one-two combination I'm waiting to drop on him." To emphasise his point he put his fists up and did a little mock shadow boxing before tucking into some more sweet potato.

"Monica, don't worry, you'll get used to it. It's like a lunatic asylum here," Veronica reassured.

Trevor gave his wife a loving kiss on the neck.

"She's right, but the patients are harmless, so long as we

get our medication regularly."

It was the sort of homely good-natured occasion that makes you feel good to be part of a tight family. The conversation was entertaining and amusing, the food delicious and the atmosphere was far removed from the everyday struggle and strife out on the streets of the city.

For a moment in the hubbub of conversation Michael found his mind drifting away from the dinner table to the future. His life was so different from those there. The freedom of a single person's life was what he had chosen, but now suddenly at this moment, seeing them all here, the restrictive shackles of commitment didn't look so bad. Could they be right and he wrong? Maybe, but did he have it in him? Could he hack it as a father and a husband, or would he drown in the suffocating, restricting waters of a conventional relationship?

> I've just been to see my best friend,
> he's found another girl.
> Says she's just about the best thing,
> in the whole damn world.
> And he says,
> can't you see what the little lady's done for me?
> He says it like he thinks I'm blind.
> But things that I see,
> ain't necessarily the things he can find.
> Oh, those happy loving couples always talk so easy.
> Happy loving couples always talk so fine…
> Those happy loving couples ain't no friends of mine.

The lyrics from a song came into his head and he was desperately trying to remember the connection. He knew the words well but he couldn't recall where he had heard it. Then it came back to him. Saturday afternoon in a woman's flat and the next door neighbour was playing the same record over and over again. The flat was in Lewisham. But he had forgotten the girl's name and exactly what she looked like. Strange, he thought, he could remember the words to a song but not the person he was with when he heard it.

Diane gladly accepted Michael's offer to help clear the plates from off the dining table. Conventional as their mum was, Mrs Hughes had raised both her sons to know that the domain of 'man's work' also included the kitchen. Their father had complained that she'd turn the boys into *maama* men, but she insisted that they should know how to cook and clean for themselves. As a result, Josey was a wicked chef and often prepared the meals for the family. Likewise Michael could comfortably 'run t'ings' when it came to cooking and domestic chores. He was grateful for his mother's enlightened thinking, because not only did it make him self-sufficient, but it always impressed women when a man was both a demon in the bedroom, as well as the kitchen. As he once told Alex: "The way to a woman's panties is via her stomach."

"She's a really nice woman, you better make sure you treat her right," Diane warned him as he scraped the food scraps into the kitchen bin.

"Don't worry Di. I've come to the same conclusion as you, and this ain't gonna be the one that got away. I tell you if there was ever a woman who could attempt to mend my wayward ways that's her."

"I'm glad to hear that Michael. 'Cause you're not a youngster anymore. It's time you were seriously thinking about the future. There's nothing so sad as an old black guy who's the last swinger in town, trying to chase young girls, when all his contemporaries have raised families and moved on. If you carry on like you're doing, you'll end up becoming that pathetic old man one day."

"You're starting to sound like Josey. Hey, give me a break. When I'm ready to settle, I'll settle."

Michael tried to sound cool but he was feeling pissed off with Di. Where did she get off telling him how to run his life? But that was the way she was. She spoke her mind. All the same it was his life and he should be free to live the way he wanted to. On his fridge at home in Blackheath, there was a post card with the message: 'You only live life once. But if you do it right, once is enough.' Damn true, he thought. But when it came to his life, he would decide what was 'right'.

Diane realised she'd gone too far and apologised. Michael smiled and told her it was 'no problem'.

In the lounge, Marcus and Bianca were both vying for Monica's attention. Marcus was showing her how his transformer toy changed from a racing car into a robot, but Bianca thought that her Barbie make up set was much more interesting. For once the two children decided that this operation required mutual cooperation. Bianca remained silent while her brother did his product presentation and in turn he did the same when Bianca sold the benefits of her doll's accessories.

Michael came and joined Monica on the sofa and Marcus was delighted. At last here was someone who would really appreciate his racing car.

"Now you know why I ain't got no pickney," Michael turned to Monica as Marcus jumped into his lap with a thud.

"Has that been by luck or design?" she joked.

"Strickly by design thank you. This jockey nah ride wid out a saddle."

"Do you want to have children?"

"Oh Monica, I thought you'd never ask. Your place or mine?"

"No, I'm being serious. Do you?"

"My old man used to say 'all good things come to those who wait' and I agree with him. Or was it 'all good things wait for those who come'?"

"I can see that if I want a serious conversation I'd better start chatting with Marcus."

"Sorry Monica, I just need to get a bit of foolishness out my system. My brother's wife has just been giving me a talking to. She says I must be a good boy and not give you a hard time."

"Damn right too. But who says I won't give you a hard time?" Smiled Monica.

"Baby, you can give me a 'hard' time any day."

"Michael, behave yourself. There's innocent minds to protect here."

Monica and Michael looked at each other and smiled.

THIRTEEN

A John Coltrane tape was playing on the hi-fi, the lights were down low and the brandy tasted smooth. Monica threw her head back and rested it on Michael's chest to make herself a little more comfortable on the sofa. They had stayed at Josey and Diane's until 8.00pm but Monica had said that she needed to get some work done that evening so had to get moving. She'd only intended to pick up her car from Michael's then go home. But the 'one drink for the road' was making it more difficult for her to leave.

"Thank you for introducing me to your brother and family. I had a really nice time this afternoon. It's not very often that I have a proper Sunday lunch like that. My family are all too individualistic for that to happen. Everyone does their own thing, so it's nice when you get a family together."

Michael agreed. It had been a good day. He didn't think he'd enjoy it as much as he did and he wasn't sure why the vibe was so special today. Maybe he was getting sentimental in his old age.

Monica finished her drink and rested the glass on the floor. She was physically close to Michael, yet she hadn't known him long. But it didn't feel like that at all. It felt as though she had known him since childhood. Although this was only their third meeting face to face, they had spent in total quite a few hours together. Probably as much time together as some people after four or five dates she reasoned. She was working it all out in a scientific way to justify why she was sprawled out on the sofa of a man that she'd only properly met two days earlier

They lounged on the settee for a while in silence, listening to the jazz waft around the room. The back of Michael's hand slowly stroked the side of her cheek and Monica's face moved closer in response. They didn't need to say anything, the music was saying more than enough for both of them.

In a moment Monica could feel the warmth of his mouth against hers and she opened to his embrace, which started slowly but grew steadily more passionate until both could feel themselves surrendering to the passion of the moment.

Monica grasped his head more firmly and explored the domain of his mouth. The tips of their tongues teased and played with one another's sensually.

Michael's hand explored the softness and fullness of her womanly bosom. His forefinger found the centre of her right breast, the nipple gradually hardening to his touch. His curiosity demanded that he explore further and he slowly slid his hand inside her wool jumper and felt for the satin smoothness of her bra. Her nipples felt even harder in response to his touch.

For once in his life Michael was prepared to wait for his pleasures. The vibe he felt wasn't the normal 'let's get butt naked and fuck'. *I want to make love to this woman not just 'push it up'*. While he considered slowing things down, he felt Monica's hand frantically undoing the belt of his chinos and then pull ing down his zip. Then her hand was on his stiff penis, fondling it eagerly. She undid his trouser button and with a slight struggle managed to free his penis from the confines of his Calvin Kleins. With her hand gripped around the long shaft, Monica savoured the size and firmness of his manhood, caressing it slowly with one hand, while slowly unbuttoning her clothing with the other. Things were not going at the slow pace Michael had expected. The runner up front had set the pace now, and it was for him to catch up. Still firmly in Monica's grip, he too stripped carefully.

As his long fingers touched her sex he could feel how aroused she had become. His two fingers slipped easily into the juicy moistness of her pussy and moved gently within her. Her hand reached to his and acted as a guide. She worked his fingers into a more vigorous rhythm, encouraging him to be a lot firmer in his approach. She was getting very turned on.

They lay on the lounge carpet on their sides, facing each other, their tongues still exploring each other's mouths. As Monica's hand caressed his penis at a more rapid rate,

Michael's head became a dizzy mix of sexual arousal. Then she stopped, got up, and repositioned herself with her face in his groin and her pussy in his. The classic '69'. She held his penis and eagerly drew it into her mouth, savouring it like an exotic dish. Michael's cock flexed automatically as he felt her warm mouth envelop it. At the same moment, he slowly licked the length of her clitoris before sliding his tongue into her wetness. His tongue stiffened and tantalised her as it explored deep inside her. She eagerly thrust herself onto his tongue, urging it deeper inside her as she pushed her clitoris from side to side in his mouth. Her husky groans grew steadily more frantic and her body movements more wild and aggressive. She sucked Michael's dick with wild abandon and sent an intoxicating, intense waves of pleasure through him. A climax eventually enveloped her. Monica carried on riding his tongue until she could take no more and then she drew away from his mouth.

Michael knew his time was near. Monica's left hand tickled his penis while her mouth moved over it's enlarged head. He felt a quiver deep within and then the start of his sexual spasms. Monica withdrew her mouth suddenly and almost immediately felt the warm gush of his semen on her chin and neck.

Monica lay on her back, gasping for air, as the physical exhaustion from their frenetic session hit her. Michael lay face down on the carpet next to her, his arm around her waist.

"Well Michael, it's nice to meet a man who knows his tongue isn't just for talking. Phew! Thank you."

"It's always nice to hear a satisfied customer," he joked, cuddling up closer.

"Shit, is that the time already?" she cried out, looking at her watch and rising to her feet at the same time. "Sorry Michael, I'm gonna have to go."

"Monica. You gotta be joking, you just can't go like that."

His words fell on deaf ears. Monica was already dressing. Michael reluctantly got up to put his clothes on.

"I thought you would stop the night?"

"I would love to, but I've got a report to prepare for a meeting tomorrow morning."

She grabbed her handbag and gave him a quick kiss on the lips before heading for the door. Michael followed her downstairs and opened the front door. Again she gave him a quick peck on the lips before climbing into her black Golf GTi parked in front of his house.

"Thanks for everything. Phone me in the week, lets have dinner one night. Bye."

With that rushed goodbye she jumped into the car and zoomed off down the road.

Michael watched her go then slowly closed the door. In the hall he leaned against the closed door. He reflected on the evening and for the first time in his life, he suddenly felt used.

FOURTEEN

Dear Michael,

Having a wicked time out here so have decided to stay on for another four weeks. So don't bother going to the airport as arranged. Will phone or write with details later about date I'm coming back. Not bothered about the job. They can sack me if they want.

Missing you lots.
Love
Nadia
PS It's very hot here.

Michael studied the postcard one more time before tossing it into the kitchen bin. The announcement of Nadia's extended visit was welcome news. It would give him some much needed breathing space while he sorted things out. He wondered what had happened to Jackie. She'd not phoned him in the last couple of weeks and when he'd called her at work that lunchtime, they had said that she was away on holiday for the next two weeks. He phoned her home, but just got the answerphone. He wondered if she was pregnant after all and had taken the time off to sort out an abortion. Although she had said that she would keep the child if pregnant, he doubted that she would. No, he knew her too well *Jackie likes her freedom too much to be tied to a baby*. She had probably gone to a clinic and was getting herself back together, he figured.

He looked at the clock on the kitchen wall then checked the red snapper gently cooking under the grill. From a small plate next to the cooker he brushed some sauce onto the fish and tossed on some more onion rings.

He really didn't want this evening to happen but he'd been caught off guard by the telephone call. He'd taken the easy, short term option and agreed to meet her this evening but he was now regretting his weakness.

He looked at the clock again. It was nearly 9.00pm. One

thing you could say about Shantelle was that she was reliably unreliable. Always exactly an hour late. He had told her 8.00pm so he figured that she would be there any moment now.

He wondered what her attitude would be like this evening. It was hard to judge what was going through her mind when they had spoken earlier. She didn't sound annoyed about his obvious avoidance of her, but maybe it was the calm before the storm. Either way, he'd find out soon enough.

There was a knock at the front door.

Shantelle was the sort of woman who always dressed up even to pay the milkman. Michael took her coat, trying to figure out whether the slick black dress was for his benefit. If she had dressed specially it meant she had definite plans for the night. The question was did Michael want to play ball?

With a kiss she handed him a bottle of his favourite Australian wine.

"It's nice to see you again, stranger. I thought you'd gone into hibernation," said Shantelle in her sweetest, good-humoured voice.

Michael felt uneasy. What was her game plan? Why was she being so nice? Was this the same woman who had cursed him on his mobile, as he sat dining with Monica the other night? *Something's definitely going down.*

"Yeah baby, I'm sorry. I've really been so busy at work that I've had to put everything else on the back boiler for the moment," Michael went on the defensive. "I was going to phone you this weekend, but I was so vexed with you girl. I think you owe me an apology."

"What for?" Shantelle seemed puzzled.

"What for? I'm at dinner with a really important Japanese client and you start cursing me out. I felt so shamed. It was bad enough the phone ringing in the first place. In Japanese culture, it's the ultimate insult to ignore your guest. To answer a mobile phone in their presence was like a slap in the face. You cost me a big deal by your feistiness."

If there was an Oscar going spare, Michael would have had the unanimous vote of the Academy. His display of outrage was totally convincing and left Shantelle feeling dejected.

"Sorry Michael. You sounded so awkward that I just thought you were with a woman. I didn't think…"

"That's your problem Shantelle, you don't think. If you'd been sitting next to Mr Hirohita of the Ju Jit Su Corporation with a £400,000 deal on the table, you'd feel awkward if some silly cow phoned up at the wrong time."

£400,000? Perhaps the figure was a bit high, but he was in full flow now and rather enjoying his own performance. *If you're gonna bullshit, do it in style* he reasoned.

"£400,000 you cost me. Fucking £400,000!" he stormed, pointing an accusing finger in front of her face for effect. "Hirohita looked at me like I was some uncultured nigga when you carried on, Shantelle. From then onwards I knew I'd lost the deal."

He spun around, turning his back on her. It had worked, Shantelle was worried and upset. He felt a touch on his shoulder. "Don't bother trying to sweet me up, Shantelle," he said, shrugging her hand off. "Four hundred grand, Shantelle. My brother has a wife and kids you know, he needs every penny he can get from the business to look after them. Then you blow it for us. You might as well cut those kids' throats." His voice boomed across the room. This was good stuff: 'cutting the kids' throats'.

"I said I was sorry Michael," she offered apologetically.

"Sorry don't pay the bills, baby. Now you know why I don't have time to see you. I'm having to work my butt off just to keep up with the runnings. I get a big break and you fucking blow it for me."

Michael marvelled at how a spur of the moment decision to bluff Shantelle had grown into a most inspired strategy. He'd read an article in a magazine which stated that it was easier to get people to believe massive, incredible lies than smaller more mundane ones. People could relate to little fibs, but not bigger ones because they would never have the boldness to do such a thing. Now he was believing it. He turned to face a tearful Shantelle and made his next move.

"To be honest Shantelle, your behaviour on Friday night really put me off. I thought, if you can't have a woman who will support you, what is the point? You understand? To be honest I felt like phoning you back and just cutting things dead between us."

Shantelle's head was slightly bowed. She had never seen Michael so angry before. In turn, Michael's performance was so convincing that he started to feel angry, believing for a moment that she really had cost him £400,000.

"Michael, I'm very sorry for any harm I've caused. I can understand how you feel, but I didn't mean to mess things up."

"Yeah right. That's the sort of line I could hear the Captain of the Titanic saying."

Shantelle looked puzzled again.

"Titanic? What's Star Trek got to do with this?"

Michael sat at the table trying not to let his feeling of smugness become visible. He picked at the fish now in front of him in an exaggerated manner, looking like a man who was pissed off. Shantelle tried to make small talk, but Michael was determined to carry this performance through to the end. He grunted occasionally in reply to her questions and made no attempt to get involved in her one-sided conversation. Shantelle nevertheless tried to lighten the mood, hoping he would eventually come round.

The meal finished, Michael poured himself another glass of wine.

"I'm not being rude Shantelle, but you can't stop over tonight. I've got work to do in the study. I'm having to put in a lot of extra hours to make up for that lost deal, you know." He couldn't resist it.

"Sure, I understand. I won't hang about and get in your way." She sounded disappointed, but wasn't about to argue with him.

Michael was in his element. This was the ultimate power trip and the definitive test of a salesman's skills. Shantelle's explosive personality was under his control and he was loving it. It was now time for the finale. Holding his finger tips to his temples he grimaced, as if a sudden pain had gripped him.

"Are you okay, Michael?"

Groaning in mock agony, he peered through squinted eyes.

"Oh man! This real bad migraine has just come on. I've had a few attacks recently."

Such was his dedication to his new-found 'method' acting craft, that he even went as far as swallowing a couple of paracetamol tablets to give his painful migraine a more believable edge.

"Excuse me Shantelle, I've got to go and lie down for a moment. It's the only way this blasted pain goes away."

Clutching his head, he stumbled up the stairs, with a quick glance back to see Shantelle's anguished face follow his every step.

He sprawled himself out on the bed and lay there for fifteen minutes, trying his hardest to hold back his laughter, before Shantelle came to join him in the darkened bedroom.

"Is there anything I can do for you?" she asked with a genuine note of concern in her voice.

Michael groaned and lifted his head.

"Maybe a massage might help take some of this tension out of my back," he suggested.

Returning quickly from the bathroom with a small bottle of massage oil, Shantelle helped him remove his shirt before playing her Mary Seacole role.

"I don't want any oil on the duvet. Could you get a large towel from the bathroom?"

The moment Shantelle stepped out of the door, Michael's mobile on the bedside table rang.

"Hello… No, I'm at home, just reading."

Shantelle called out from the bathroom, enquiring about

what colour towel to fetch. Her voice was audible to the caller, but Michael covered his tracks.

"Oh no, you're not disturbing anything. I've got someone here fitting new curtains. I can't decide if I should have blue or white ones."

At that moment Shantelle walked into the room. Michael hurriedly put his hand over the mouth piece. He quietly mouthed something to Shantelle which she took as 'Mr Hirohito', the important Japanese contact.

"I'll have to phone you back later as I'm in the middle of sorting this out. No when I said I was reading, I meant I was going to do that later."

"Yeah speak to you in the week, Monica."

Michael realised his slip as soon as he said it and could tell from her look that Shantelle heard it clearly.

"Who's Monica?"

Michael had already sorted out his escape route. He looked at her puzzled.

"What Monica?"

"You said on the phone 'see you later in the week Monica'." Shantelle was indignant, throwing the towel onto the bed.

Michael held his side and burst into laughter.

"Oh Shantelle, didn't you ever go ah school? I said 'Moneeka'. That's Japanese for 'lickle more'. Sometimes you really amaze me, Shantelle. Now I see why the government want to sack so many teachers."

Shantelle was now running on the defensive.

"Alright Michael, you don't have to be rude. They didn't happen to teach Japanese at my school, alright?" she said with a frustrated sulk on her face.

Michael wondered if there were no limits to Shantelle's gullibility. Suddenly, he could feel the actor coming out again. He lay down and held his head in pain.

Having first spread the towel down, Shantelle got busy with the oil. First, she applied some liberally to her hands, warming them with her breath. She then rubbed it firmly into his broad, dark back. Her sensual fingers moved their way around his back, making long strokes from the base of his spine up to his neck.

"Oh yes, that feels much better," he told her.

Such was the effectiveness of Shantelle's magic fingers at removing his tension, that Michael decided that her sphere of influence should be widened to include territories not presently explored. He undid his belt and button and slipped his trousers and boxers off. Smoothing more oil on to his lower back, Shantelle let her hands wonder at will, caressing new areas of firm, flesh. The palms of her hands massaged lower, the oil running down into the valley of his strong muscular buttocks. Shantelle's touch lingered long enough on his behind for Michael to realise that she was having wholly inappropriate thoughts about his firm, pert bottom.

With her proven dexterity, her silky fingers stroked his sensitive inner thigh. His penis stiffened further with her every touch. The temptation was too much for him to bare. He rolled onto his back to free his penis. It hardened further, enjoying its new found freedom. Like a mighty black staff, his cock stood tall and erect.

Shantelle, knelt on the bed, looking down at his penis and smiled. With slow, deliberate movements, her crossed arms gripped the sides of her dress and pulled it over her head before tossing it over her shoulder. She was obviously prepared for the evening as she wore nothing beneath the silk dress. She stood astride him, a foot on either side of his stomach.

"Now that's what I call a view," was Michael's saucy remark.

"Behave yourself you naughty man," she teased, playfully rubbing her foot against his stiffness.

Shantelle recognised that wicked, enigmatic look in Michael's eyes and knew what that smile meant. She stood over him, stroking her clitoris with her right index finger and opening her pussy lips for him to sneak a glimpse. Standing over him gave her a sense of power. She felt like a lioness about to devour her prey.

"Michael I need satisfying now," she declared. "I need that strong cock of yours inside here," she murmured in a husky voice, opening her pussy wide to make her point. He pointed to the bedside table, where she knew the pack of condoms was always kept. Taking the rubber sheath in her fingers, she slowly unrolled it along the throbbing firmness of his wood. Then with feline grace, she lowered herself onto his penis, inhaling sharply through her teeth as she accommodated him inside her.

The sensual odour of sex permeated the dimly-lit room and a spirit of wild abandon gripped the two of them. Leaning forward, she lifted her pussy up from his cock until the tip of his head was at the entrance to her mound. With care she lowered herself down onto him, before rising again. Having repeated her prelude, she noted Michael's mounting excitement. She rocked backwards and forwards, her movements becoming more frenetic, her mind slipping into a deeper sensual state. She stared at him hard in the eyes, the smouldering look of lust etched clearly on his face. Her expression was serious.

"So you want me to fuck you, do you?" she cursed. "Is this how you wanna be fucked, Michael? Do you wanna be fucked hard like this? Yes. Is this how you want it? Your cock wants me to fuck it hard, doesn't it Michael? Oh yes Michael! That's it. Oh yeah, oh yeah, oh yeah! Oh Michael, I'm coming! I'm coming!!"

A gorgeous, intense orgasm shook her body and provoked a scream from deep down inside her. Her climactic moan was enough to trigger Michael. As she slumped forward onto his chest, he gripped her bottom tight and pumped his seed into her.

As he lay on the bed resting, his mind drifted to Monica and for an inexplicable reason, he began to feel guilty for sleeping with Shantelle. Monica would be annoyed if she knew what he was doing at that moment. He knew her type; she wanted a straight, no-messing kind of relationship. Sexing Shantelle was certainly not conducive to that.

He really did like Monica, a lot. He couldn't think of any

woman he'd met that he'd taken a liking to so quickly. He wanted her to be more than an occasional sex thing, which meant he'd have to behave himself. He couldn't see himself giving up sexing other women completely, he was only human after all, but maybe he could cut down the number and perhaps he could be more discreet about it.

His contemplation was halted by Shantelle who was busily getting dressed.

"Well if you've gotta work, I suppose I'd better leave you. I don't want you saying that I don't support you."

In the excitement, Michael had forgotten what he'd told her earlier. He breathed a sigh of relief that she was leaving. Now he'd had his pleasure he really didn't want her around taking up his space. He slipped on a bathrobe and showed her out the front door. He made himself a coffee.

"Mr Hirohito! The fucking Emperor of Japan. God, that bitch is stupid." Michael burst into laughter. "What a fool she is."

He finished his coffee and read the newspaper. He yawned; it was time to hit the sack. As he switched off the light, the phone began ringing.

"Hello Michael, it's Barbara here. Just thought I'd give you a bell to see how you are. I've been thinking about things and I realise that I've been crowding you too much. In short, if you wanna see me then that's up to you. I can't force you to do anything. If you don't, then I'll have to live with it. At the least I hope we can still be friends. That's it. It was just a quick call to let you know.

Okay, well I'll speak to you soon. Sweet dreams, Michael."

Michael listened to the answerphone message. He was pleasantly surprised. He had been worrying that Barbara was going to get all dramatic and make life difficult for him, but she seemed to be playing ball. She sounded happy and reasonable about things. He decided to give her a ring the next day. Now that they were no longer an item, he might just visit her in the week.

FIFTEEN

The bedroom window was half open and a late night breeze was gently blowing the white lace curtains by the opened sash window. In the corner, a small night light burned on the pine chest of drawers, casting a star-shaped shadow across the room. From the front room, a Bach violin concerto played on the CD player.

It had been a nice session of passionate sex with Barbara and Michael was slowly coming around. He looked to his side, but Barbara wasn't there.

The session flashed back to him. Barbara licking his cock and balls like a woman possessed and lying on the bed with her legs around his neck as he rode her deeply. Oh it had been wild, but he was paying the price now. His dick hurt bad.

He heard the bedroom door open wide and turned to see Barbara walking in with a tray. She placed it on the bed and smiled.

"A stud needs to keep up his strength," she smiled.

On the tray was a glass of orange juice and a plate with a piece of buttered, hard dough bread, salad and potatoes and what looked like a sausage next to it. He picked up the knife and fork and pulled the tray closer, casting a hungry eye over the appetising dish.

A soul-wrenching scream filled the room as the tray and plate flew through the air and crashed onto the bedroom floor. With petrifying fear in his eyes, Michael pulled back the duvet and saw that he was lying in a lake of crimson wetness. He stared in horror at the mutilation that was his severed penis. He let out a scream that could wake the dead and heard it echo through the darkened rooms of the house.

The street lamp outside cast a bright orange glow into the room as Michael shot bolt upright and frantically wrenched the duvet from his bed. He stared down at his flaccid penis, then let out a sigh of relief. It was still there, exactly as he had left it when he went to bed a few hours earlier. Again he looked, just to make sure. He breathed another deep sigh of relief as it dawned on him that the whole thing had been a terrible dream.

Sweat trickled from his brow. He lay his head back on the pillow to reflect on the worst nightmare a man could ever have. Not given to having dreams, let alone unpleasant ones, he was all shook up. *How could a dream be so real?* He asked himself the question over and over. He went through the details of the nightmare again, trying to explain it. Was he feeling guilty about Barbara? In his subconscious did he think that he'd treated her badly? Was it linked to Monica and his indiscretion with Shantelle? He mulled over all the options and decided he was wasting his time. *Everyone gets a bad dream sometime.* He needed to be up early in the morning. Pulling the covers over his head, he tried to get back to sleep.

SIXTEEN

Josey looked at his watch and checked the boxes and delivery note again. Everything was correct and he could see no problems. All the shipment notes were in order and the van should be there at 3.00pm. He'd phoned and checked the flight arrival times and the 9.00am flight from Moscow was on time. If all went to plan, Michael should be arriving with Ivan Andropov at any moment now.

It had only seemed like a few days before that the Russians had first visited, but four weeks had passed already and February was almost March.

The deal was coming at the right time, Josey reflected. The £40,000 deal would save their bacon as things had been going so bad of late. This and the DeBorchgrave Publishing contract should get them back on their feet.

Josey had been amazed that his brother managed to get work from DeBorchgrave Publishing, as he knew that the company worked with a major computer supplier. But Michael was persistent when it came to selling, even though he had been evasive with details of how the deal was secured. With a signed order for twenty grand's worth of equipment, Michael could be as evasive as he wanted, Josey reckoned.

"Here comes trouble," Cynthia announced.

Josey turned round to see Michael outside, with Ivan in tow.

"Greetings comrades," Ivan joked as they entered. He paused to give Cynthia's hand a gentlemanly kiss.

After the initial pleasantries, Ivan explained that Michael's influence was being felt in Moscow.

"Bad boys inna London, rude boys inna England. Down in the jungle, yeah yeah."

To Cynthia's amusement, Ivan was attempting to sing, in his broad Russian accent, a jungle hit by UK Apachi.

"Your brother buy music tapes for us last time. Da? Much liked in Moscow. I have sell many copies," Ivan informed Josey.

Michael's new role as 'cultural ambassador' caused much mirth among the others.

After Ivan had checked through all the equipment and documents, he produced a wad of US dollars and counted out the agreed amount. Josey disappeared to bank the money, while Michael entertained their guest. He had something to check with the visitor.

"I hope you don't mind Ivan, but I've arranged with the local newspaper for them to send a photographer down today to take a photograph of us." Michael mimed with his hands, someone taking a photograph, for the Russian's benefit. "They are going to be writing a story about us. 'LOCAL BUSINESS SECURES RUSSIAN DEAL'. You know that kind of thing. It will be good publicity for my business."

The Russian nodded his approval. Cynthia laughed at the very slow and precise way Michael was speaking.

"Jus' rest yuhself," he teased. "At least when I chat, him can understan' we. Not like some street gyal I could mention."

"Cho'. Better 'im don't understan' me, than I talk like a bleeding dalek," she scoffed.

Ivan looked baffled.

"Do not worry, Ivan. She is what we call, 'feisty' in our language."

Poor Ivan didn't have a clue what was going on, but nodded his head and smiled in a gesture of understanding.

Cynthia kissed her teeth.

"That's nice but could we move in a bit closer? Yeah. That's nice. Hold it." The man clicked and took his final photograph. "Thanks very much. I'll be on my way"

The photographer's visit had been perfectly timed. The delivery van was pulling up outside the shop to take the equipment to Heathrow, when he arrived.

When the driver had loaded the last of the cases onto the van, Ivan bid his farewells to the staff of Mac In-Touch and climbed into the van's passenger seat.

"Come visit Moscow, comrades. You very welcome. Goodbye, or as they say in your country, 'leekel more.' "

Ivan waved his farewells and the van merged into the slow moving traffic of Kilburn High Road.

Back in the shop, Josey had some concerns to voice.

"Mikey, do you think this newspaper story is a good move? I was thinking that it might be stirring things up a bit. You know those people at Micro Chippie are gonna hear about this article? They're already gonna feel vexed about being skanked with the Russians. This is kinda rubbing their noses in it."

Michael pondered the matter carefully, weighing up both sides of the argument, before giving his considered verdict.

"Fuck those Micro Chippie pussies. If they wanna play rough, we can do the same. They already tried fucking us up with the cops. This is legit so we don't need to worry. Let them see the story. Anyt'ing they can do, we can do it rougher. Fe true, amigo."

Josey wasn't convinced, but it was done now, so there was little point in worrying.

Michael looked at his diary and worked out the figures. It was exactly 37 days, 11 hours and approximately 45 minutes since he first met Monica. It had to be love, otherwise why was he doing this foolishness, counting hours and days? If someone had told him five weeks ago that he'd be so into a woman as he was with Monica, he'd have laughed. If this wasn't love, then love didn't exist. It had been such a long time since he'd liked a woman this much that he couldn't even remember her name.

He couldn't quite explain his emotions. Maybe it was because she had all those qualities he wanted in a woman. Or was it because she had appeared at a time when he was questioning his whole bachelor status? Here was a woman who was good-looking, intelligent, amusing, sexy, sophisticated and yet down to earth, classy, and entertaining. Yes, here was someone he would be proud to call 'my woman'.

It didn't mean he intended becoming a monk or anything like that. He was after all a man, and what normal man could be truly faithful to one woman? But he knew where his heart lay and that was all that was important right now.

Over the last few weeks he'd dated Monica many times and it would have been more, he thought, but she was always tied up with work. Still, on those times when she was busy, there were other possibilities if the need struck him. He had dealt with Shantelle last week, but he didn't want that 't'ing' becoming too regular. He kept telling Barbara he'd meet her "next week," but then something always seemed to come up. Still she wasn't going anywhere. He had phoned Jackie several times to no avail and was still without information on the baby situation. All he could do was wait for her to make the next move. All in all everything seemed to be going very well at the moment.

The crowd in the Galleries Wine bar was the usual mix of City workers enjoying Friday evening drinks to see in the weekend. The Holborn wine bar was not far from Monica's office and was a good place to meet up before deciding which restaurant to eat at.

At 8.00pm on the dot, Monica walked into Galleries and spotted Michael at the bar. She kissed him warmly on the lips and pulled up a stool. He held her close to him and kissed her again.

"Mmmn. We should meet more often," she purred.

He ordered a glass of white wine and another bottled lager.

"It's good to see you, Monica. You're looking criss."

They sat and talked through the entertainment options for the evening but could come to no definite decision.

"To tell you the truth Michael, I'm feeling a bit tired. I wouldn't mind just getting a takeaway and sitting in front of the TV."

"Yeah. That's cool with me. Why don't we go back to my yard and I'll get us a Chinese."

"You have a deal."

An hour later, they were pulling up outside Michael's home. Monica relaxed in the front room while Michael brewed up some tea then prepared to leave again to collect their meals from the Chinese takeaway.

"Make yourself at home, I'll only be about five minutes. I've left the answerphone on," he called out to her as he departed.

Monica stood at the window, watching Michael's car pull away. She stared idly across to the pub on the other side of the road where the 'thank God it's Friday' revellers were becoming more boisterous. She was about to turn away when she caught sight of a shape in the shadows. As she looked closely, she made out the figure of a black woman staring directly at her. It was too dark to recognise her features, but the woman appeared to be wearing a long, dark coat and a headscarf concealing much of her face. The woman stood motionless.

Drawing the curtains, she stepped away from the window and switched on the television. Perhaps the woman was just waiting for someone in the pub. 'Stop being paranoid', she told herself. Monica, nevertheless, felt uneasy about the mystery woman.

The slam of the front door hailed Michael's return. He darted into the kitchen to unpack the meal. Placing the assortment of foil containers on a tray he carried them into the front room, with a large carton of juice and two glasses.

"There's some woman across the road who seems very interested in this place, Michael."

He looked at Monica quizzically then walked to the window and peered out into the darkness.

"Where?"

"By the pub."

Monica came over to show him, but the woman had gone.

"She was right over there."

Michael smiled and started humming the music from 'The Twilight Zone'.

"Maybe it was your mother checking up on what her daughter is doing," he joked.

"Now why didn't I think of that? It's the most obvious explanation." Her sarcasm was cutting. "By the way did you ever find out who those early morning visitors were?"

"No. They didn't come back, and I'm not sorry I didn't find out. They looked like a couple of pitbulls, man. I sure wasn't going to be asking them what they wanted."

"Maybe they were the henchmen of some gangland boss whose daughter's honour you besmirched," she teased.

"Now why didn't I think of that. It's the most obvious explanation."

"Touché."

"Come on, let's eat or this food is going to get cold," he said.

After the meal Michael poured a couple of brandies. They sat cuddled up, watching a made-for-TV movie about a haunted house.

"Cho'. Now you tell me what woman is going to go down into a dark cellar with a lickle torch, 'cause she heard a sound like someone being strangled? Chupidness!" Michael observed.

"But Michael if the woman was to simply leave the house and call the police, we wouldn't be sitting here watching this 'cause there wouldn't be a story and, therefore, no film."

"Lawd have mercy. Me sorry me opened my mout'."

"You make me laugh, Michael. If nothing else, you're good for a laugh."

He came closer to her and kissed her slowly on the lips.

"I hope that's not all I'm good for," he said softly.

"Well, maybe I can think of a few other uses."

They cuddled and relaxed themselves in the cosy ambience of the softly-lit room.

"You know Monica, I'm really enjoying things between us and I'd like it to continue. You know, for things to get kinda deeper between us."

"That's a nice thing to say. You know I like you a lot,

Michael and enjoy being with you and I'm sure things will get deeper if that's what we want." She turned to face him. "I meant to ask you this before. Are you seeing anyone else? I mean, are you sleeping with anyone else?"

"Listen baby, right now there's only one woman in my life and she's sitting here, next to me."

"While we're asking the questions, maybe I should put the same one to you."

"No Michael, there is no other man in my life at this moment. Happy?" She said.

The flame of the candle flickered gently near the bed. The classical music playing softly in the background matched the mood of the evening perfectly. Michael back on the mattress, feeling mellow as his penis slipped smoothly into her mouth.

"Oh yeah baby, that feels good," he murmured.

Her mouth sucked hard on his member, the pace quickening. Then she playfully bit the shaft of his dick.

"Hey, slow down a bit," he cried. "Oi! Stop, you're hurting. Hey, didn't you hear what I said? Ahrrrrrrrgggggh!"

Michael's head shot up, his face twisted in excruciating agony, to see Barbara's blood-smeared smile. In between her thumb and forefinger, she gripped his severed penis by the tip of it's foreskin.

Michael's frightened jerk was enough to wake Monica from her slumber.

"What's happening? Are you alright?"

Michael lay gasping for breath, his forehead glistening with beads of cold sweat.

"Michael, what's the matter?"

"Sorry, baby. I just had a bad dream. Yeah, sorry to wake you. I've been having these terrible nightmares over the last few weeks. They're so real they scare the shit out of me."

"What happens in these nightmares?"

"Oh uhm… I imagine I'm in ah… uhm, what you call it? Car accident… And I get badly hurt."

"Well that could mean anything. They say dreams are often a way of the sub-conscious dealing with different fears, doubts, or guilt."

"I don't care what the theory is behind it. I just want it to stop. This thing is making me scared to go to sleep. They seem to be getting more frequent as well."

"Maybe you should go and see a therapist."

"Don't be silly. You saying I'm mad or somet'ing? I don't need no therapist, I just need to slow down from work. That's all."

"Hey, don't be so touchy. Just because you see a therapist, it doesn't mean you're mad."

Michael sunk his head deep into the pillow and gazed up at the ceiling as he tried to calm himself down. The dreams had been worrying him a lot and the last thing he needed to hear was that he was going mad. He could clearly remember as a boy, his Uncle Cecil changing from an easy-going ladies' man into a paranoid, crazed person who believed that kitchen utensils were trying to kill him. His Uncle spent a number of years in a mental hospital before committing suicide when Michael was a teenager. The memory of his personality change haunted Michael to this day.

He had tried to work out what was causing the dreams but couldn't reach any firm conclusions. They had simply started one night and had steadily got worse. Now they were occurring a couple of times a week. The theme was always the same, but the story different. Barbara would always end up removing his manhood in some cruel and horrible way during or just after sex. He prayed that the nightmares would stop. If they got any worse he would have to go to a therapist or he surely would go mad.

"Try and get some sleep Michael and don't let it worry you," Monica told him, resting his head on her chest before nodding off again.

But Michael couldn't sleep. He lay wide awake, staring off into the distance wondering what these horrible nightmares meant.

After a couple of hours, during which he'd tried in vain to sleep, he decided he might as well get up. Despite being very tired, he was feeling restless. *Maybe a snack will relax me.* He made his way to the kitchen where he poured out a bowl of cornflakes and went to get the milk from the fridge.

His heart skipped several beats and his body jerked back a pace as he pulled open the door. Then he looked again and breathed a long sigh of relief before breaking into a smile. The thick salami sausage on the shelf smiled back at him. *I must be more tense than I realised.* His tired mind and active imagination were playing tricks on him.

Monica stirred from her sleep a few hours later. Dressed in Michael's bathrobe, she found him busy at work on the computer.

"And I thought I took my work seriously. 9.00am on a Saturday morning. I am impressed." She walked over to his chair, wrapping her arms around his neck and kissing him on the top of his head. "Are those dreams still troubling you, Michael?"

"No, I'm fine now. I had to get some work done so I thought I'd get an early start. What can I get you for breakfast?"

"Oh just some coffee, and toast with your rather handsome willy on top."

Michael jumped up from his seat. He couldn't hide his anger.

"Don't say slack things like. It's not funny, alright? Please don't say that."

"Michael, calm down. I was only joking. And what's this rubbish about slackness. That's great coming from the man who asked me if I like chicken, then whipped out his willy and said, 'well suck on this, it's really foul'. Come on, Michael."

Michael laughed and hugged her.

"Did I really say that old chicken line? It must have been someone else."

"No Michael, all the other men I know are gentlemen." She hugged him back, "That's why I like you. It's your lack of sophistication I find so appealing."

They went to the kitchen where Michael rustled up some saltfish and egg with hard dough bread and they sat at the kitchen table discussing plans for the day.

"Well, you know, I'm supposed to be meeting my mate Alex at the gym this morning. I could phone and blow him out if you wanna do something."

"No, that's alright, I'll come with you. I could grab a newspaper and coffee while you guys do your t'ing. I'd quite like to watch you flex yourself."

He extended his arms with his last morsel of strength, but had to concede defeat. Exhausted, Michael stood up from the padded bench and shook his head.

"I'm getting too old for this lark, Alex."

"Yeah, you should have retired years ago. I'm surprised you don't have a walking stick yet, dreadie."

"So much for support from friends. Don't forget you ain't no yout' no more neither."

As ever the Saturday morning banter was the piss-taking that both men enjoyed indulging in.

"Hey Alex, you know this woman I've been talking about, well she's in the café. You can meet her later and then you'll know why I tell you that this lady is special."

"Mikey, I worry about you. You're starting to sound soft in your old age. What happened to the 'love 'em and leave 'em, break their hearts and deceive 'em', hombre?"

"When you meet her you'll know why I'm mad about the girl. Anyway, don't worry, I ain't gonna give up my t'ings. I'm just moving into the undercover lover stylee. You understan'?"

Alex patted his spar on the back and joined him in a conspiratorial chuckle.

"That's what I like to hear my man. For a moment I thought you were turning into Luther on me," grinned Alex.

After a rejuvenating shower, the men casually walked into the cafe.

"Alex, this is Monica Bramble. Monica, this is Alex Short-ass."

Alex didn't appreciate Michael's introduction but he had other things on his mind.

"I've heard so much about you, Monica, it's good to finally meet."

Monica looked up from under a borrowed Nike cap and shook his hand cautiously. "I'm sorry to hear about your accident."

"Accident? The woman was lying. I'm definitely not the father."

Michael jumped in before his friend put his foot in it.

"That's Alex, always the joker." He winked his eye at his homeboy. "Remember when we went down to see that client of mine in Brighton a few weeks ago and we had that accident in your Saab coming back? Well as a result, I missed a date with Monica."

"Oh that accident," said Alex. "No, the damage has all been sorted out now. It was no problem."

Michael wasn't yet sure if he'd got away with it. He looked at Monica to see if she believed him, but she seemed a million miles away. Anyway, there was nothing she could positively prove about his cover-up. Even if she suspected, she'd still have to give him the benefit of the doubt.

They sat down and Michael went to order some juices. He looked over briefly to see Alex and Monica deep in conversation. He was even floating his arms around for emphasis, his white gold identity bracelet streaking through the air. He was glad that they got on. It was always good to get your spar's seal of approval when it came to a new woman. He would hate to have one of those situations where you're always reconciling your best mate and your woman.

Michael returned to the table with the drinks and various snacks.

"I can see what's made my spar go so ga-ga in the last few weeks," Alex complimented Monica. "Michael has good taste, much like mine. But then again I am his mentor."

Monica smiled. "So you're the man I should thank? He's learned his craft well. You must be a good teacher," she joked, searching deep into his eyes.

"Well at the University of Love, where young Michael was a student, I wasn't just a don, I was the head don to rahtid."

Monica laughed.

"Oi, oi, oi! Break it up. Ignore this man, he's just plain nasty," Michael interjected.

"Aye, aye. What d'you mean 'plain'?" Alex challenged.

Alex used every new meeting as an opportunity to do business. Reaching into his wallet he pulled out a business card and handed it to Monica.

"If you or any of your colleagues need a mobile phone, just let me know. I'll give you the best deal in town."

Monica slipped the card into her handbag. "Someone at work was talking about getting a mobile so I'll pass the card on."

"Please, anyone else you can think of just get 'em to buzz me."

Michael stepped in to break up the hard-sell.

"Alright, Alright. Enough rude bwoy. Don't harass the woman."

"It's no problem, Alex." she reassured him.

After twenty minutes of humourous conversation, Monica popped off to the bathroom, giving Michael the chance to get the 'SP' from his friend.

"What d'you reckon? She's nice isn't she? Now you see why I keep going on about her?"

Alex smiled in agreement.

"Yeah, I can definitely see why you're hot on the woman. Nah man, she's... ah... safe. Seriously nice. Yeah, a well-criss gyal, or I should say 'oman?"

"That's what I was telling you, roots. Now you know why I haffe keep t'ings undercover. Monica's pretty straight about things, you know dem weh deh? She wouldn't be cool about me checking other women. But as they say, 'what dem nuh know, nah hurt dem'."

Michael spotted Monica coming through the cafe doors so he quickly changed the subject.

"Typical. I could have known you two would be talking about computers. Why can't you be like most men and talk about women? Or did you have that conversation when I was out?"

"Yeah. During the five minutes you were gone I asked Michael to tell me his whole sexual life history. It was such a short story that we had to move on to computers," teased Alex.

"Now I know you're lying. We'd be sitting here in three months time if you asked him that question," Monica jested.

"This must be the 'Let's Take the Piss Out of Michael Day'. Give me a break, people. You know I'm a very sensitive soul."

Monica squeezed his cheeks and gave him a kiss.

"Ohhh, poor baby. Is everyone being nasty to you?"

"Well folks, I hate to break up the party, but I've got to sort out some runnings," Alex announced. "Monica, it was a pleasure meeting you. Mikey, more time."

The two men touched fists and Alex departed, leaving Monica and Michael enjoying a coffee at the café table.

"I'm glad you like Alex. He's a real laugh-a-minute kind of character. Good for when you need to get that dinner party going with a swing. If you can get him any business I'd appreciate it. Things are a bit rough for him at the moment."

Monica looked at her watch and seemed deep in thought. Michael sensed her anxiety.

"You gotta be somewhere?"

"Uhm, yeah. I've got to get back home and do some work. If you could drop me at the nearest tube station, I'll take a train."

"Nah man. I'll drop you there."

"No really Michael, I don't want to inconvenience you. The tube will be fine."

"Don't bother arguing. I ain't letting you catch a tube when I have a car. Anyway I fancy cruising around this morning."

"Well if I'm not putting you out, that would be great."

It had looked from first light as if rain was only a dark cloud away and sure enough the heavens opened. Monica held Michael close to her, and using her newspaper as a makeshift umbrella, dashed across the sports centre car park to Michael's car. Within a moment they were inside, shaking the rain off their clothes. As they pulled out into the main road, the downpour thundered down thick and heavy.

After a few minutes drive they were on the motorway by Hackney Marshes and heading south to the Blackwall Tunnel.

"It would be nice to go away for a weekend. What about Paris or somewhere like that?"

Monica beamed at the idea. "If anyone mentions Paris, you know I'm definitely saying 'yes'. The only thing is, I'm a bit tied up with things at the moment. Maybe next month or something. Is that okay?

"No problem. That would be nice," he assured her.

Despite the rainstorm, the Saturday midday traffic to South Wimbledon was much better than they had anticipated. Michael pulled up to the curb outside her house and switched off the engine. He held her close and gave her a slow lingering kiss.

"It was a nice evening, night and morning, 'nuff respek for everything."

"I had a great time too. Take care of yourself and I'll see you in the week."

Michael had driven a few miles away into Tooting and was waiting at a set of traffic lights, when he noticed Monica's matt black electronic address book on the front passenger seat. He turned the car around and headed back to south Wimbledon to return it.

Monica looked surprised to see him when she opened the front door. Michael explained the reason for his return and handed her the electronic organiser. As he started to walk back to the car, he stopped and turned to her.

"Yah know, I hope that one day I'll get to see the inside

of your yard."

It had dawned on Michael that, for whatever reason, he had never been invited inside her place. She'd told him that it was a mess and needed decorating.

"Michael, come round for dinner at the weekend," Monica called after him. "I'd invite you in now but there's someone from work here who's working on a document with me."

Michael nodded his understanding.

"No problem. Check you in the week. Laters."

On his journey home, a nagging doubt started to creep into his mind. Was Monica embarrassed about him? Was that why she didn't want her work colleague to meet him? *Maybe I'm getting paranoid.* This woman was really getting to him. If this was what love felt like, maybe he didn't want it after all. Why was he being such a wimp?

This is Michael Hughes here. She's only a woman. Anyway, which woman in the past has not wanted me? They've all loved me bad. So why should this one be any different?

His ego gradually built his confidence up again and by the time he'd reached his yard he was back to his usual state of mind and ready for the evening's entertainment. He sat on the lounge floor and dialled a number from his address book.

"Hi Sandra, it's Michael here... Yeah, I know. It's been a long time. Listen, what've you got planned for this evening?"

SEVENTEEN

He could sense trouble and decided that today he'd deal with it head-on. As Michael stepped out the front door, he noticed the men getting out of the blue Vauxhall Cavalier parked across the road and walking towards him. They were too burly and mean-looking to be cops, so who were they? He recognised the two white bruisers as being the same ones who'd made the early morning calls a few weeks ago. He quickly worked out possible strategies in his head. He could floor the first with a punch to the jaw, but what about his partner, would he be able to take him out too? Then again, they knew where he lived and would probably come back and things could get worse. He decided to play it by ear. As they got closer he stiffened himself for action.

"Michael Hughes?" asked the younger, cockier one.

"What's it to you?" he replied in his meanest voice.

The young one handed him some papers, which he took. "What's this?"

"You're a bloody difficult man to get hold off. It's a court summons for non-payment of your poll tax."

Michael was belligerent, but relieved.

"There's gotta be some mistake. I'm sure I paid it ages ago."

The job done, the bruisers were disinterested and started back to their car.

"You should speak to the court about that," the other man shouted as he unlocked the car.

Michael was actually happy to be given the official document, it could have been worse. The absurdity of it amused him and he smiled as he pulled away in his BMW.

When he arrived at Mac In-Touch and saw Josey's face he knew it was going to be one of those days. His brother grunted "hello" and called him into the back office.

"Did you see the article in the Kilburn Gazette?" asked Josey passing him the newspaper.

'Big Macs to Russia' said the headline. 'Local computer firm lands Moscow deal', was the sub-heading below.

Michael read through the story then looked at his brother.

"What's the problem? You don't look too ugly in the photo."

Josey kissed his teeth.

"You always haffe make joke. There's nothing wrong with the story but I told you it would stir things up."

Josey handed him an unfolded sheet of white A4 paper.

With individual letters cut from newspaper headlines, the warning was clear: 'If you play with fire, you gonna get burnt'.

"What's this foolishness? Real theatrical, innit? Josey, you ain't seriously worried about this, are you? Those wankers at Micro Chippie are just trying to wind us up. I told you what that batty bwoy said when I was at Brands Hatch. The guy knew all about the police visit. They set us up. Don't bother about it. There's nothing they can do."

Michael was blasé about the whole thing and was slightly annoyed that his brother was taking it so seriously. *How could he allow those wankers to get to him?*

"Look Mikey, there are people out there who would like to see us fall. You know how people stay. They see you with your own business and they're jealous. You can't take these things lightly."

The brothers discussed the matter for some time. Josey felt that Michael was being cavalier and flippant in his attitude, whilst Michael felt his brother was carrying on like a maama man and fretting too much about nothing. What was done and past help was past grief. They would, as ever, just have to watch their backs.

Michael checked his messages with Cynthia before making his round of calls.

"Yeah, and can you call Mike Bailey from Prima Graphics? And a woman called Barbara phoned. Said you had her number. And someone called Rupert something, Debauched?"

"You're not far off. Deborchgrave?"

"Yeah that's it. He said would you like to come to dinner

at the weekend?"

Michael kissed his teeth. He'd had his fun with that situation and got some business out of it, but he had no great interest in repeating it.

"Can you phone him back and say I thank him very much for the invitation, but I'll be away on business this weekend?" he told her.

"Okay. That's all the messages. But your car insurance runs out in a couple of days time. Do you want me to renew it?"

"Cho'. A year gone already? No it can wait, I don't have the money at the moment. I'll sort it out in a few weeks time."

"You shouldn't drive without proper insurance, you know. Maxi was telling me about a time when he had an accident without insurance and it cost him a fortune and a lot of hassle."

"Oh, Maxi says, does he? So Cynthia, you've being checking out Maxi Fabulous?"

"I've been out for a drink with him, that's all. I don't think checking is quite the right word... Yet." A huge grin appeared on her face. "Nah. He's gonna have to work for it. What I've realised from people like you Michael, is if a guy gets it too easy he don't appreciate it. That's life. You enjoy things more if you have to work for them."

"Go deh, Cynthia. You're learning the game plan quick, ain't yuh?"

"You have to. But seriously, behind all the macho stuff Maxi's really quite a nice guy with a very sharp brain. He's just got a bit wrapped up in playing a role, that's all. But with a good woman at his side, like me, I'm sure we can straighten up the poor, mixed-up bwoy."

"Cynthia Fabulous. Yes it has quite a ring to it. If I don't get a wedding invite, I'm gonna kick up stink. Yuh know dat."

Cynthia kissed her teeth.

At lunchtime, Michael made his way to McDonalds, picking up a copy of 'The Voice' newspaper on his way. Over his regular McChicken meal, he glanced through the personal pages. He seemed drawn towards a particular ad:

Madame Dupre
Spiritual Adviser
Specialist in dream reading, fortune telling, spells
and other spiritual matters
All major credit cards excepted.

Michael examined the ad again and looked over his shoulder cautiously. The last thing he needed was for someone to see his interest in such services. His curiosity was already aroused however, and he considered dialling the number.

Ordinarily, he would have dismissed such an advert as 'foolishness', but these were not ordinary circumstances. Yet again, 'The Nightmare' had kept him up all night long. He had to do something and maybe that something had to be on the spiritual tip. If nothing else it would be an experience. Desperation had never been in his vocabulary before; it was making a memorable debut.

Looking over his shoulder again, he dialled the number on his mobile. It rang for quite a while and he was about to end the call when a woman's voice came through the earpiece. He couldn't quite place the accent, but there was definitely a hint of French. He assumed she was from some part of the Caribbean.

With his hand cupped around the mouthpiece, Michael quietly explained that he was having nightmares and needed help. The old woman listened sympathetically to his predicament and suggested that he come to her as soon as possible as it sounded serious. She lived in nearby Hampstead and was available that afternoon. Michael decided that now was as good a time as any. He shoved the remaining half of the chicken burger in his mouth and hurried from the restaurant.

After returning to the office and informing Cynthia that he had a business appointment, he set out for the address, indigestion gripping his chest. *Why do I have to be so craven? Couldn't I leave that burger? Damn.*

Half an hour later, he was outside the house. Selby Avenue was typical of roads in the area. Small, terraced houses, all well-maintained and identical. These once humble artisan's cottages were now expensive homes for successful writers, actors and business executives. Number 6 was graced with neat terracotta window boxes and a dark green front door with shiny brass fittings.

No wonder the ad said 'all major credit cards accepted'. Business was obviously going very well in the spiritual world. *I wonder if she needs an Apple.*

Walking through the opened small, cast iron gate, Michael's finger hovered over the antique door bell. Before he could press it, an elderly black woman opened the door.

"What the f…!"

Dressed in a long, white linen dress with a matching head scarf, the brightness of her clothing emphasised the darkness of her skin. She smiled and welcomed him into her house.

"You must be Mr Hughes. Please follow me. Don't be afraid."

Visibly shaken by the doorbell incident, Michael followed her nervously. *What the fuck am I going in for?*

It was nothing like he was expecting. A small quaint house, the rooms were painted in the same pastel yellow and furnished with an impressive collection of antique oak furniture, mixed with African artifacts. The old woman led him into a small back room. The room's heavy, green velvet curtains were drawn and the only illumination came from an old oil lamp resting on a small circular table in the centre. The room was so dark that he couldn't quite see the back wall. Two small wooden chairs sat on either side of the table. Madame Dupre´ knew how to present her business just right. The image was so perfect that even a cynic like Michael could become a believer.

She showed him to his seat and joined him on the other side of the table, the dark shadows across her face from the dimly-burning lamp adding to the surreal ambience of the room. The words 'duppy' and 'dyam fool' sprang to Michael's mind.

"My name is Madame Dupre´. I was born in Haiti where the ancient spiritual teachings of our African ancestors were passed down to me as a young girl. They said I had the gift. Many are called, but few are chosen. I charge £50 for consultations lasting up to an hour, thereafter I charge at a rate of £30 an hour. Medicines, spells and potions are extra. All prices are subject to VAT at 17.5%. Now my dear, please tell me the whole story." She was frank and to the point.

Michael steadied his hands and wondered how he was to phrase the situation. He did not relish telling a 70 year old woman that he was having nightmares about his cock being severed during oral sex.

"Well Madame Dupre´, I uhm, keep having this nightmare where terrible things happen to my, uhm, body."

"Please Mr Hughes, be more specific."

"Well, uhm, I imagine that I've made love to an ex-girlfriend and I then realise that she has removed my, uhm, uhm organ."

"Are you referring to your heart, kidneys, liver, or penis, Mr Hughes?"

"Well, ah-uhm, the last option."

"How is your penis removed, Mr Hughes?"

"Well, by a knife and, uhm, other things."

"What other things, Mr Hughes?"

"Well, uhm, her teeth."

"Is this woman giving you head at the time?"

Does she have to make this so difficult?

"Well, uhm, uhm, yes."

The old woman closed her eyes and said nothing for a moment. Michael scanned the room. Things were no more visible than before. Madame Dupre´ opened a wooden box on the table and removed a pack of cards. She fanned the cards out in her hand and offered them towards Michael.

"Pick a card."

Michael's slightly shaking hand reached towards the centre of the pack and withdrew his selected card.

"Turn it over," Madame Dupre´ instructed.

For a moment she pondered the illustration of a woman holding a dagger. Michael sat stunned, staring at the upturned card. A bead of salty sweat trickled into the side of his mouth. Fear consumed his mind as he failed to come up with any answers to explain his selection.

"The meaning is clear. A woman wants to cause you harm. You must be very careful as you are in danger of falling into the depths of insanity if this continues. You must put a counter spell on this woman."

"The dream I'm having is about a woman called Barbara. She must be the one," Michael reasoned.

"No. It is not that simple. Dreams can be a mask to hide many things. She may not be the one. You must be sure who is responsible or the dreams will not stop."

"But how do I find the person responsible?"

"Think long and hard about who would want to do you harm. Then try and find the evidence."

"That's the problem. I can't think of which bi… I mean which woman, would want to do anything bad to me." *All my women departed satisfied judging from the smiles on their faces.*

Michael pondered the matter then reached for his wallet.

"American Express?"

"That will do nicely, Mr Hughes."

EIGHTEEN

"Hello darling, give me a big hug."

Monica wrapped her arms around his waist and gave him a tight squeeze. Michael responded by planting a kiss on her lips. As he stepped forward his eyes surveyed the hallway.

"There ain't nothing wrong with this place. What d'you mean it's a mess and needs decorating?"

Monica's home was a picture. The through-lounge was styled in beige and cream and had a very Scandinavian feel about it. A great deal of time and money had obviously been spent on designing the house, with the modern, designer interior in total contrast to the 1930's exterior.

"Yeah, this is a real dump. I don't know how you've got the front to invite me into this place," Michael said sarcastically as he walked around the lounge, checking out all the details and admiring the features. "Yeah. I like these radiators. They're like a work of art on their own." He had seen the same radiators in a shop in Kensington when he was decorating his place. He couldn't afford them.

"So Monica, did you do all this yourself?"

"Well I got someone to design it. I showed him what I wanted from a book."

"You must be a valued asset at work. Those people are obviously paying you well."

Monica looked embarrassed.

"Well my father helped me out financially with buying the place and the improvements," she explained.

"That's the sort of daddy every girl should have. It was money well spent, though."

While Michael carried on admiring the decor, Monica went to the kitchen to pour out a couple of glasses of wine. She checked the oven and started to prepare the rice and accompanying salad. She had cooked a traditional Greek Moussaka, with fresh minced beef and aubergines and peppers. When everything was under control, she joined Michael in the lounge, where he was flicking through her records.

"I know where every single one of those records should be, so don't even think about nicking any."

Michael turned to face Monica with the two wine glasses in her hands.

"As if I would." He replaced the rare Isley Brothers album.

"Cheers." She raised her wine glass and touched Michael's. "Michael, you're looking tired. Are you sleeping alright?"

"So-so. To be honest those dreams are still bothering me."

"I told you, go and see a therapist."

Michael hesitated for a moment about whether he should tell her about his visit to Madame Dupre´ on the Monday. He decided he might as well.

"I have to admit that I went and saw a woman about it." He flopped in the sofa.

"What sort of woman?" Monica enquired, slipping next to him.

"Well, a spiritualist."

"A spiritualist. Do you believe in that stuff?"

"Well, you know. I thought I'd just check it out for myself. For the experience. At the time it seemed convincing, but thinking about it later, I thought 'hang on a sec, this woman makes a living from this shit'. She's probably suckered more people than some of the best scam artists out there. She walks away with £50 and knows that I'm going to keep coming back until it's sorted. But there you go, it was at least an experience."

"If you look at it that way, I guess there's no harm," said Monica. "Except the criss new shirt you could have bought with that money." She couldn't resist rubbing it in.

The meal was soon ready and they sat down to eat in the slightly-raised dining area. The rectangular marble and glass table and high-backed chairs fitted in well with the overall high quality design of the house. The table's glass top especially amused Michael.

"You certainly couldn't play with yourself at a dinner party in this house," he joked.

"You're so nasty. And over dinner as well."

"That's me. Nasty by name, nasty by nature," he rapped.

"Baby, don't give up the day job," Monica teased.

She topped up his wine glass and went to change the music on the hi-fi. In the lounge, she suddenly froze in her tracks.

"So how's your brother and family?" she called out, her eyes fixed.

"Oh Josey's freaking out at the moment. We've had a couple of threatening letters at work and he's taking it all a bit too seriously. We had one on Monday and another on Thursday."

Monica hadn't heard a word of it. Her eyes were focused on something glistening under the sofa cushion.

"Some rival computer firm trying to be hard men," Michael continued.

Monica knew exactly what it was and knew Michael would, too. She walked slowly across the room, towards the sofa. The visible 'X' becoming larger and louder in her mind.

"What are you doing out there? Don't you want to know what we're going to do about them?"

"I'm just looking for a particular CD. Keep talking, I'm listening." Monica moved the cushion and pushed the article further out of sight.

"Everyone I've told that story to always asks the same question, 'What did the letters say?' On the other hand you just wanted to know our next move. That shows a mind that doesn't want too get bogged down in the details."

"Wow. And I thought I was the one who was supposed to have the psychology degree. That's some heavy analysis." Monica's voice became more amplified, as she skipped into the room, satisfaction beaming across her face.

"When it comes to you, Monica, I just love probing you, baby."

"You are such a disgustingly rude man, Michael. That's

why I like yah, chuck."

Michael gave her a lingering look then leant across the table and kissed her. The kiss was passionate and full of lustful urges. She gave him a saucy smile and sipped her wine provocatively.

"I know this is bad timing, but I really need to visit the lickle rude bwoys room."

"Up the stairs, second on the left. Don't be long."

As Michael climbed the pine staircase, Monica exhaled a huge sigh. She couldn't afford to be that sloppy again; too much was at stake. Meanwhile, Michael was investigating her bathroom. Like the rest of the house, attention to detail was the style. A tasteful white bathroom with chrome and glass fittings, it was minimalist chic. Michael's attention was drawn to a small, silver-framed photograph by the side of a potted fern plant near the window. Taken on what looked like a tropical beach, the photo was of Monica and a white man in his mid-forties. With greying hair, he had the distinguished look of someone who didn't have coal miners for cousins and had a lot of money. Monica looked almost the same as she did now and Michael wondered when the photograph was taken. Who was the man?

It made him think. He didn't know that much about Monica's recent past. He'd never really asked her much about her previous relationships but he came to think about them now. He wouldn't blame her if she wasn't forthcoming. He tended to be deliberately vague himself when it came to ex's. Once a man starts to mention more than half a dozen names, a woman starts to suss out that he eats Pedigree Chum. He knew women well enough to know that Monica wasn't the fooling around kind of girl. Slack, she certainly wasn't, but what *was* her past?

He zipped up his flies and flushed the toilet. As he turned off the tap and dried his hands, his eyes were still fixed on the photograph.

Out on the landing, his gaze perused the bookshelf positioned between the two bedrooms. There were several books on architecture, which surprised him as she'd seemed so disinterested in the work on the house. The biggest surprise, however, was the books on the bottom shelf. A number of new and old books on witchcraft and spiritualism. For a woman who had such an interest in the subject, she seemed very dismissive of him seeing Madame Dupre´. *All these questions and very few answers.*

"I thought you'd got lost up there. I was about to send out 'International Rescue' to track you down."

"Sorry, I was just admiring the decor up there. Very Corbusier, that bathroom."

"My, we do know our designers, don't we? I didn't know you were interested in design, Michael."

"Hey, I might be a bit rough around the edges, but it doesn't mean I don't have a brain, you know."

Monica could sense that something was annoying him.

" 'Why have I got a picture of myself hugging up some white guy in my bathroom?' Am I right?" Monica read his thoughts and seemed to enjoy beating him to the punch.

"Yeah, it did cross my mind."

Monica was silent for a moment.

"I'd actually forgotten that it was still there. It was only when you went up that I remembered."

Michael kept quiet, waiting for the rest of the answer.

"He was a guy I met a few years ago and we had a relationship for a short time. That photo's been there for a long time. I never got around to taking it down. Does it bother you?

"No. Why should it?"

"I know that a lot of men don't like to see photos of a woman's previous partners. And I wondered if the fact that he was an older white man, bothered you?"

"Don't be silly. I'm not that insecure. It don't matter to me if the guy was white or black. We all have a past so why should I get annoyed about seeing one of your old boyfriends?"

"Well, that's not the entire story."

Michael looked puzzled, waiting for the next clue to unravel the mystery. "Think about it, Michael. What was the name on the order form from my firm?"

"Monica Bramble." Michael looked almost insulted by her ridiculous question.

"No, try again."

Michael scratched his beard. He abruptly stopped as the revelation dawned on him. Monica nodded in recognition of the inevitable.

"*Mrs.* Monica Bramble." The words trickled out of his mouth.

"Would you like some coffee?" Monica asked, breezing into the kitchen, closely followed by her shocked guest.

"Excuse me, don't you think the fact that you're married is of some importance to me."

"Michael, you've slept with married women before." Monica spoke with her back to him.

"Ah come on. That's unfair, I…" Disbelief filled Michael's voice.

"I know, I'm sorry. The fact is we are 'legally separated' and he hasn't lived here for ages. It's history. His picture is still in the bathroom to remind me that he was a shit part of my life. Okay?" Monica was becoming emotional.

Michael still couldn't believe how an idyllic evening had transformed so drastically. He turned and returned to the table, wishing he hadn't mentioned anything.

In the past, the one thing that put him quickly off a girl, was when she started having an attitude about his ex partners. He certainly didn't want to come across like that, and regretted showing that it bothered him. But married, that's another kettle of fish. *Isn't it?* With women, it was always best to play it cool.

He got up again and walked slowly back to the kitchen. Monica hadn't moved an inch from the position he had left her in a few moments ago. He wrapped his arms around her, resting her head on his shoulder.

"Your past is your past, Monica. All I care about is the present and the future."

Monica lifted her head, showing her tear-streaked face. She gave a short smile before burying her face into his chest.

As the evening wore on, the bad vibe was forgotten and Michael and Monica were back to their usual jokey selves. After consuming another bottle of wine, they played an unusual version of Blind Man's Bluff. Using a woollen hat and a head scarf, Monica blindfolded Michael in the kitchen then hid in the lounge where he had to find her. The game was made more exciting by the fact that both players were totally nude. If Michael could locate her within a minute, oral pleasure was the prize. If he failed to find her within the time span, he would offer her similar services.

His first time out of the kitchen with the unfamiliar surroundings, Michael failed to make the one minute allowance, so he paid the forfeit. Monica sat giggling on the sofa, her legs wide apart, while Michael eagerly devoured her.

By his second attempt, Michael was getting the hang of the game and easily located his target in good time.

It was now Michael's moment to seize his prize and he sat triumphant.

The playing eventually had to stop and the couple spent the rest of the evening exploring each other's bodies on the lounge carpet. Michael kept his blindfold on, adding to the sensual thrill of the moment. His hands wandered over her body fondling her breasts. In a short time, he had entered her moistness and with his cock stiffening at every thrust, she wrapped her legs around his waist and made him give it to her hard and long.

"Fuck me good."

The aggression shocked and aroused him at the same time. Michael tried to hold on, but felt himself contract and his sperm shoot into her.

"Oh you bastard!" she cursed at his early arrival. Pushing him off, she forced his head to her sex and made him tongue her to a frantic climax.

When they had caught their breath, Michael removed his blindfold, scooped Monica up in his arms and carried her up the stairs' where they collapsed on her bed.

NINETEEN

The barman returned and set the two bottles of beer on the polished wooden counter. In Islington's trendy Cuba Libre, the atmosphere was extremely lively for a mid-week night. Decked out like an authentic Cuban bar, the venue was a cosmopolitan mix reflective of the area's trendy inhabitants. Everyone was out for a good time. Everyone except Alex.

Michael couldn't figure it out. It was totally out of character for Alex to be in such a glum mood and even stranger for him not to say what was bugging him. Michael had asked, but got a terse 'I'm alright' in reply.

This was supposed to be a buddies night out, but Michael was beginning to regret it. He passed the beer to Alex and started on his own.

"So Alex, is business alright?"

"Yeah man, it's not too bad. Could be better, but it's the same for everyone."

"True, true." Michael reached into his jacket pocket and pulled out a velvet jewellery case. "Hey, check this my man," he said opening the case to display an impressive gold chain. "I bought this as a little somet'ing for Monica. I'm telling you it must be love. This is the most money I've ever spent on one gift for a woman, yuh know. Three hundred notes, rasta."

Alex examined the necklace and slowly shook his head before sipping his beer.

"You're crazy Mikey. £300?"

"You're right, I am crazy. But the woman's worth it. I saw her last week and I'm telling you, the time we had. Bwoy, if you were there, you'd know why I say she's worth it."

"I can't believe I'm hearing this fuckries from Michael Hughes, 'the original Sexelero', remember? Mikey you hardly know the woman and you're doing foolishness."

"Alex, you're wrong. I know the woman, she's an angel."

"Yeah right. She's the same as all the rest of the bitches. And you're a fool if you think different."

The last remark didn't go down well with Michael, but

he was willing to forget it. He and Alex were like brothers. His spar always had his best interests at heart. Maybe Alex was pissed off because he had lost his bracelet. He didn't even take his cargo off in the shower, so he looked decidedly naked without that gleam around his wrist. He didn't want to vex him any further by bringing it up.

"Alex, don't speak about Monica like that. This woman is special to me, rasta."

"Mikey, how do you know this woman ain't a *ginal*? You pull enough skanks with women, how do you know the same ain't being done to you?"

Michael figured that Alex was worried about losing a drinking and raving partner. Men always got that way when one of the fold decided to settle down.

"Look, I've known a lot of women in my time. I've met them all. I know the way women stay. Monica ain't like that. And even if she was, so what? I like the woman and that's all I care about."

Alex reflected that he'd gone a bit too far and decided he should let the matter rest.

"I understand what you're saying Mikey and it ain't none of my business. But all the same, I think you should tek care or else you gonna get burned."

Alex's last words of warning made Michael listen up. The menacing note that had recently been sent, sprang immediately to mind, but from his friend's face, Alex hadn't made the connection.

"That ain't an expression I wanna hear at the moment," Michael replied, reminding him about the note. His spar looked embarrassed on realising what he'd said.

"True. I forgot all about that business. Sorry, no offence meant, Mikey," Alex apologised .

Michael was glad to know that his mate was concerned about his welfare and didn't want to create a bad vibe. Changing the subject, he steered the conversation away from Monica and started talking about the attractive shape of the bottom gracing a girl standing near a cigarette machine across the bar. Alex checked it out for himself and conceded that he "could deal wid it".

"Anyway Mikey, what you doing looking 'pon gyal batty so? I thought you were practically married to your darling Monica?"

Alex enquired with a wide grin on his face.

"Don't take the piss. You're speaking to the hearticle sexelero. This is one gunslinger who has no intention of ever hanging up his gun, star. I just can't lick shot like them earlier wild west days, that's all," Michael jokingly hit back.

"Well boss, when you ready to ride again I just hope you can still hit the target," replied Alex laughing.

"Don't you worry 'bout dat. Ah me name bad bwoy Josey Wales, seen?" Michael laughed confidently.

For Michael and Alex this was what Friday nights were all about. An escape from the pressures and stresses of trying to keep your head above water in the Monday to Friday rat race. Friday was the night a couple of guys could go out, have a few laughs, 'check de gyals' and generally chill. It was time for man 'an man to sit down and reason with what was happening in the crazy world out there.

Michael was glad to have the time to escape from the immediate pressures he was under. Of late he'd been feeling that the pressure in the cooking pot was getting a whole heap too high for his liking. Tonight he wanted to forget about the stress and pure distress he'd been handed out in the last few weeks.

Once again it was the sight of female form that interpreted the attention of the two men. Their eyes were transfixed on the two tall sexy black women who had just walked in the door. Dressed in trendy 'club' style clothes, the women had the look of models and carried themselves in a way that said they were used to getting attention.

They strolled up to the bar and ordered a brace of cocktails. The woman in the leather trousers and matching black jacket put a cigarette to her mouth and searched in a small handbag for a light. Michael made his move. With a deft flick of his thumb he sparked a flame to life and extended his hand towards the cigarette.

She smiled politely and thanked him.

"Yeh I like the style. You two models?" Enquired Michael moving into chat up mode.

"Thanks." The leather-clad girl was polite but clearly not interested in getting involved in any conversation. She collected her change from the barman and walked back to an empty table near the door with her companion.

Michael smiled and nodded as he watched the backs of the women move away from the bar. He looked over to Alex and made his assessment.

"Them two is game. They jus' playing hard. Believe me rasta. Leave it a few minutes and then we'll make our move. Jus' watch the ride selecta."

Michael was confident that he would be pulling tonight but his spar was not a believer.

" You sure 'bout dat? The girl didn't look too interested. You know how some of these stuck up West End girls can stay. It look like them t'ink them is too nice," replied Alex who clearly was not feeling too confident of their prospects. He spied over his shoulder at the two women sitting at their table giggling together. They certainly looked well fit but Alex could see they were the sort who were used to getting attention and were too sussed out to fall for any corny lines.

Michael had other ideas. Having checked out with the barman the type of cocktail the women had previously ordered, he carried a glass in each hand and began the walk to the other side of the wine bar's polished wooden floor.

He'd got halfway across when two hip-looking white guys wondered in and spotted their dates. They went over to the women's table and hugged and kissed their respective partners. The party had clearly arranged to go on somewhere else and the women got up ready to leave.

Stuck in a no man's land in the middle of the bar Michael pretended that he had intended to go to the toilets in the first place. As a guy exited the toilet and looked puzzled as to why someone should be entering the gents with a couple of drinks,, Michael could hear the raucous belly laughter of Alex echoing from across the room.

TWENTY

Another blast of foam finally killed the last lick of flame and the fireman stepped back after he was sure that the fire had been finally laid to rest. The intense light that had bathed the surrounding houses in a warm orange glow, vanished as the flames died away. The local residents — many clad in their night attire — took their cue and started to drift back to their homes. The show was over. The rest of the fire crew started to load their equipment back onto the fire engine and prepared to get underway.

"You'll have to get this removed in the morning. If we'd got here a minute later the petrol tank would have gone up and it might have set all these other cars alight."

The fireman's words passed right through Michael without having any impact. He sat on his front doorstep dressed in a T-shirt and boxer shorts, staring at the burnt out shell of a car that was once his gleaming BMW. His bare feet rested on the cold ground but he wasn't aware of the chill that gripped the night air. A state of shock held him in a hypnotic vice-like grip.The fireman recognised the familiar signs and decided it was best to leave the unfortunate owner with his own thoughts. He turned and headed back to the fire engine whose blue strobe lights had now been switched off.

Michael tried to pull himself together but the same thought stayed locked in his head. His insurance had expired. His goddamn car insurance had expired. Why the hell hadn't he found the the money at the time to renew it? What the raas was he going to do? He had no car but still owed a small fortune to the finance people. How could he afford to get another motor and still pay off what was owed on it?

He couldn't remember ever feeling so totally gutted in his life. His BM meant a lot to him. It represented all the blood, sweat and tears he had spent working at the business building up the sales. Now it lay in front of his Blackheath house looking like a pile of scrap yard junk.

As the fire engine pulled away from the scene, the remaining neighbours who had gathered to watch the spectacle, drifted away and Michael was left in solitude with nothing more than his thoughts and the cold of the night.

This smouldering wreck in front of him was the same car that a few hours earlier had brought him home from his West End drink with Alex. His last drive had been so unmemorable he reflected. If he'd known it was going to be his last trip at least he could have enjoyed it more, he thought.

Eventually the cold started to wear through to his bones and he decided it was time to head back inside and try and shut this nightmare out of his mind. Maybe if he could go back to sleep and when he woke in the morning it would all be a terrible dream. Maybe this was all a dream like the terrible ones he'd been having recently.

He dragged himself to his feet and headed back in through the front door. The shouts of his neighbours which had woken him from his deep slumber started to haunt him and he started to play back the moment when, in a half sleep, he had peered out of his bedroom window and seen the car ablaze.

'If you play with fire, you gonna get burned.' The warning messages he received recently had come home to reek havoc. Was this what the message had meant, was it a coincidence or was it only the start of something much worse? Who the hell was the arsonist? The questions had no answers and this made it all the more frightening.

Michael could feel his hand shaking as he opened the door of the kitchen cabinet and reached for the bottle of brandy. Shock had started to grip his body and he suddenly began to feel frightened and vulnerable. His mind was desperately trying to hold onto a sense of normality but a deep, dark abyss lay in front of him and he could feel himself slipping ever downwards.

As he gulped the smooth cognac down his throat he could taste nothing and the quicker he swallowed the liquor the more his body seemed to shake and sweat. After his third glass he decided to seek support in the comfort of the leather of his sofa. His body slumped deep into the settee and his head fell into his cupped hands. His head felt dizzy and his stomach queasy.

"Bastards, fucking rhatid bastards."

The words spluttered feebly from his quivering mouth as he cursed those unknown demons that had reeked this evil upon him. His voice was shaking and trembling with built up emotion. Michael didn't know if he felt like crying or fighting the world. The emotions washed through his head like the waves on a beach. One wave brought a rush of self pity but as quickly it crashed into a swirling foam of anger.

At the back of his mind was the awful thought that he knew but could not come to terms with. His car insurance had not been renewed and the smouldering, blackened mess of metal outside his house, represented seventeen grand's worth of blood, sweat, and tears that had literally disappeared in a puff of dense black smoke.

It felt as if a close friend had been murdered and his killer had vanished without trace into the cover of darkness. For Michael the BMW represented the realisation of his efforts to make something of his life. BMW stood for Black Man Working, and working damn hard. It was symbol of his success — achieved against the odds in a society where there was no easy walk for the average black man.

Now it was gone and he was left owing the finance company a whole heap of dollars and with nothing to show for it. Michael felt as gutted as the blackened steel shell that was once his pride and joy.

He kept asking himself why he'd not found the money to pay the insurance premium. The more he asked himself the question, the more sick his stomach seemed to feel. He'd gambled and lost and was now wondering why he'd been such an idiot for 'trying a ting' with the insurance matter.

During a gap in the bout of fear and self loathing, Michael dragged himself up and returned from the kitchen with the bottle of brandy. After two more heavily filled glasses, the pain ebbed slightly in his stomach.

Now his thoughts turned to revenge. He would get those bastards at Micro Chippie and he would make them pay. He was certain it was them and if it was the last thing he did he'd make them pay. They had clearly been angry about being skanked over the Russian deal and now it was pay back time.

"Well you wan' test we? Then come test we."

Michael staggered around the lounge in a drunken haze, talking out loud to an imaginary representative from Micro Chippie. His right hand gripped the neck of the brandy bottle and held it like a club, threatening his opponent.

"You fucking bastards are gonna pay. Yah hear me? You're all gonna pay."

A small marble ashtray fell to the floor as Michael's leg knocked into the coffee table on which it sat. He moved to the wall to gain some support before swaying towards the sofa and slumping face down into it's leather confines.

The clatter of the morning's post through the letter box stirred Michael from his slumber. In that fraction of a second that separates sleep from the real world, Michael wondered if it had all been a dream. But as his conscious state took over the controls, he knew that last night was reality and he was going to have to deal with it.

His eyes slowly focused on the coffee table, then moved around the room, taking in the familiar features of his front room. A sharp pain in his head began to make its presence felt as the awakening progressed. A sickly feeling from his belly let Michael know that he was the victim of one serious hang over.

The blasting hot shower and the copious glasses of orange juice had helped, but as he sat at the kitchen table gripping a mug of strong black coffee, he had to accept that he felt less than one hundred percent.

He'd earlier peered out of the lounge window — hoping that maybe his BMW would be exactly as it was when he had parked it, but it wasn't. He felt slightly more optimistic as it looked as if a new interior, glass and respray might be enough to get her back on the road. He knew enough people in the motor trade who could get it sorted for very reasonable dollars. It was fortunate that a fire engine had been close by when the emergency call went out. They had arrived so quickly that they were able to put out the blaze before a fireball had erupted from the car's petrol tank. Things could have been worse he reasoned, and maybe there was some light at the end of the tunnel.

His concentration moved for the moment onto the the black velvet jewellery case he discarded on the kitchen table. Opening up the rectangular box he looked again at the attractive gold chain inside. It would certainly look good on Monica he thought and he couldn't wait to see her reaction when she opened the case.

He'd have liked to have seen her that weekend but he remembered her saying she would be out of London on some sales seminar in Manchester. The idea to post the case through her letterbox as a surprise when she got home on Sunday night, suddenly came to him. *Yeh that might be a cool way of playing things* he thought. Rather than give it to her face and make it seem like he was were trying to impress her. He remembered Monica saying how she hated guys who tried to impress her with money or what job they did, so he reasoned that this way she'd get the right message.

The box had come with a small white message card inside and this settled the matter for Michael.

'To my Nubian princess who shines as brightly as any gold.
Much love and respect. Michael xxx'

He signed the card and carefully placed it back into the case. There was no time like the present and he had the urge to grab a cab down to Monica's house and play postman. He gulped down his coffee and looked for his wallet and keys.

He'd got to the bottom of the stairs when he remembered his usual Saturday morning workout with Alex. He slowly climbed back up the stairs and reached for the phone on the lounge floor.

He was surprised that Alex wasn't in as 9.30am on a Saturday was normally one time he could always guarantee to find his spar at his yard. Michael left a message on the answer phone saying he couldn't make it to the gym.

The ringing phone stopped Michael in his tracks, as he once again made his way down the stairs. He hesitated for a moment, deciding on whether he should answer it or keep moving. As he contemplated his decision the answer phone cut in.

"Hello Michael, it's Barbara. If you're there can you pick up the phone please."

Michael kissed his teeth and carried on walking.

"I know you're there Michael, so just pick up the phone please. Have you been sleeping well Michael? Or have you been having some some bad dreams Michael? Have you been living your worst nightmares Michael? Well you're going to keep having those bad dreams until you start treating me nicely and showing me some proper consideration and affection..."

Michael didn't hear any of Barbara's ominous message. He was already out of the front door and heading down the street to the mini cab office. Had he stopped to listen, Barbara's slow menacing, deranged-sounding tone would have sent an icy chill down his spine

The deep tones of Ragga FM's Johnnie Wonder were pumping quietly, but strongly from the radio in the living room. At the kitchen table her eyes scanned the newspaper page, looking for the final piece to complete her puzzle. At last a headline of appropriate size yielded the necessary letter 'T'.

With precise and careful application of her scissors she cut the letter out and stuck it in its correct place on the sheet of note paper. She examined the spelling of every word, each made up of letters cut from the newspaper. Satisfied, she smiled to herself and wondered what her next act of vengeance should be.

'If you play with fire you're gonna get burned.'

A broader smile came to her face as she contemplated the look on Michael Hughes' face when he opened the letter that would carry this message of impending doom.

She hoped fear would grip him at the moment of reading and he would wonder where and when the hand of the avenger would next strike.

She chuckled to herself as she recalled throwing the match into the broken driver's door window in Michael's BMW. The buzz of excitement as she ran down the road, the car's alarm shrieking in the dark of night, came back to her and made her even more amused.

She felt used by Michael Hughes and was determined that he'd pay for treating her like she was 'rubbish'. No way was any man going to carry on behind her back and act like she was a fool. No way, no how. Michael was going to pay and pay big time she told herself. Shantelle looked again at the note and kissed her teeth with a tone of self congratulation.

At that very moment, Michael's mini cab was pulling up outside Monica's neat semi-detached in South Wimbledon.

"Hold on here for a moment, I'm just going to post something through the letterbox." Michael instructed the driver.

Monica was just stepping out of the shower when she heard the familiar clank of the letterbox downstairs. With a white towel wrapped around her slender body and one wrapped around her head she looked very much like the Nubian princess Michael had described in his card.

Sitting at the small wooden dressing table in her bedroom Monica rubbed moisturising cream into her cheeks and examined her skin in the mirror. Then she remembered.

Pulling open the dressing table 's top right hand draw

she removed a man's style, white gold identity bracelet.

"This nearly got us into a lot of trouble you know. Michael nearly found it on the sofa. Men can get very upset when they find out you're sleeping with someone else." Monica's tone was sarcastic and it brought a small grin to her lips.

Monica tossed the inscribed bracelet onto the ruffled bed. From under the sheets the outline of a man made movements of life and slowly pulled the the linen from over his head. He rubbed the sleep from his eyes and peered at her.

"What? You say somet'ing baby?"

Monica carried on with her beauty treatment.

"Oh, nothing important. Go back to sleep Alex."

END

POSTSCRIPT

Jackie gave birth to a beautiful baby girl at south London's, St Thomas' hospital six months later. The Child Support Agency are currently assessing what Michael's monthly payments should be.

Barbara later appeared on the Chrystal Rose chat show during a programme about obsessive lovers and juju. Her counselling sessions are going well.

Shantelle has a new secretarial job at a large insurance company dealing with fire damage claims.

Monica moved to The States where she is head of sales at a major cable network in Washington DC. She is to marry the millionaire owner in three months time.

Alex is stilling running his mobile phone business. Even now he feels guilty.

Michael still does the dealing and wheeling at Mac In-Touch. He is slowly coming to terms with his break up with Monica and he still has bad dreams. His counselling sessions are going well too.

END